3 1172 02427 5448

PLACE MILL

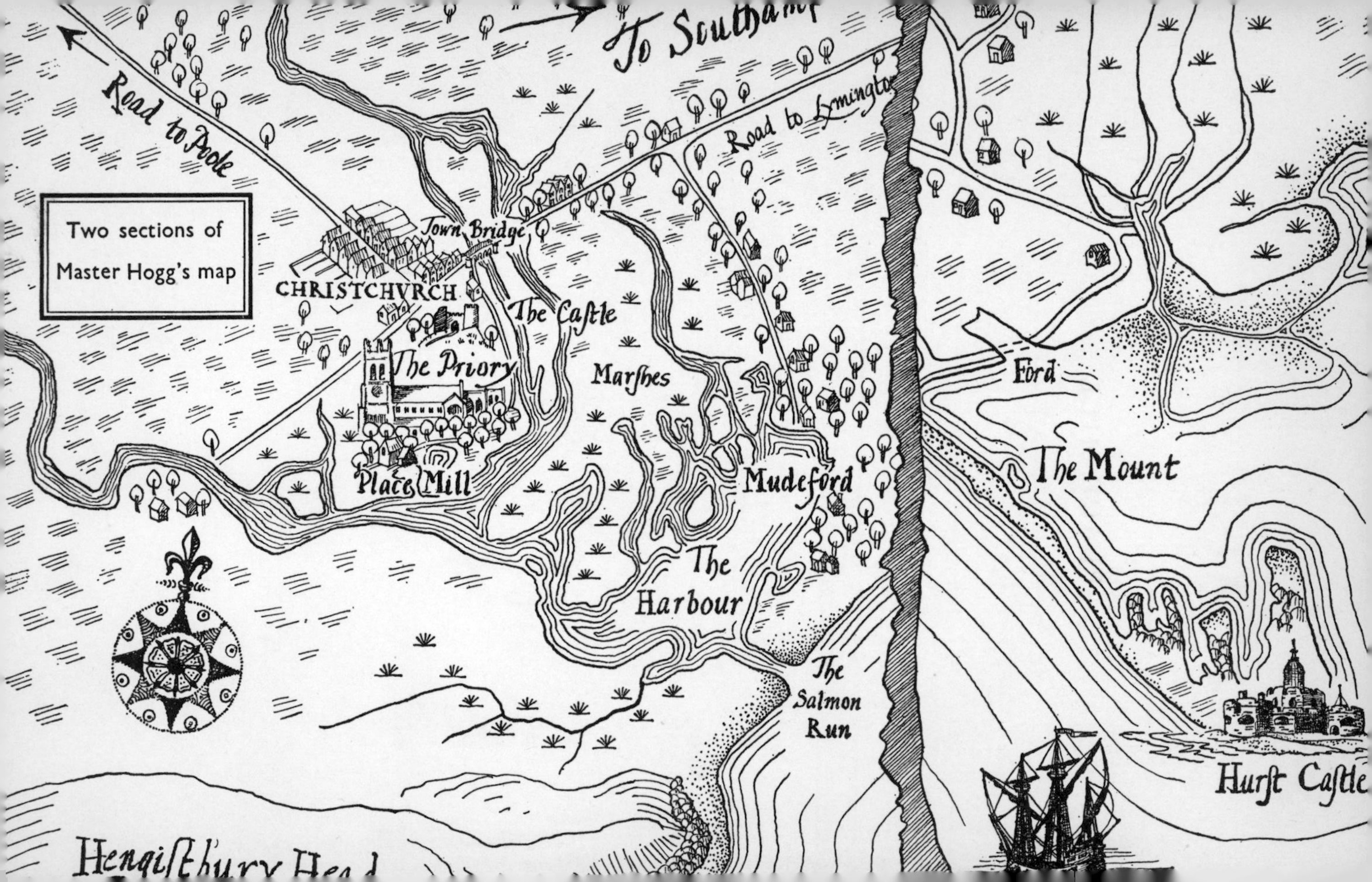

Two sections of Master Hogg's map

PLACE MILL

BY

BARBARA SOFTLY

Illustrated by

SHIRLEY HUGHES

LONDON
MACMILLAN & CO LTD
NEW YORK · ST MARTIN'S PRESS
1962

Copyright © Barbara Softly 1962

MACMILLAN AND COMPANY LIMITED
St. Martin's Street London WC 2
also Bombay Calcutta Madras Melbourne

THE MACMILLAN COMPANY OF CANADA LIMITED
Toronto

ST MARTIN'S PRESS INC
New York

PRINTED IN GREAT BRITAIN

JUV.
FICTION

CONTENTS

64-05920
325

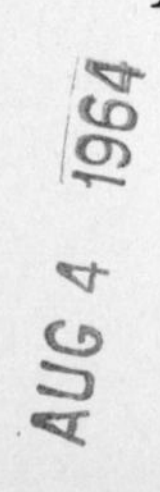
AUG 4 1964

Foreword

THIS story is set mainly around Christchurch in Hampshire, in the autumn of 1651, after the young Charles II had been defeated by Oliver Cromwell at the battle of Worcester. Disguised as a servant, he was taken through England by his friends, and finally he escaped to France from the obscure village of Brighthelmstone—Brighton—in the October.

At that time, Christchurch was a little fishing port, which had only been involved occasionally in the Civil Wars. After one battle, in 1645, which was fought all over the Priory grounds, Parliament voted the town thirty tons of oak to repair the damage.

Place Mill was one of the three mills mentioned in Domesday, and it is the old name of the disused mill on the Quay, now built below the Priory. Because it has changed and has figured so little in local records, I have based it, to a large extent, on the mill which is still worked by water power at Yafford, in the Isle of Wight.

Master Hogg's map has been based on the map of the area for 1698, when an attempt was made to use the harbour for larger vessels. Although the shape of the harbour and the position of the salmon run at Mudeford have altered over the years, the view from Hengistbury Head must be much the same, from Poole to the Isle of Wight, and towards Hurst Castle outside Lymington.

I am very grateful to:—the miller of Yafford, for allowing me to explore his mill, the Curator of the Red House Museum, Christchurch, for information regarding cargoes in the harbour, and the Epsom and Ewell Public Library, for invaluable assistance in obtaining books and a copy of the map.

Chapter I

The Swing

WITH a stab of her toe in the ground, Katharine sent the swing sharply into the air. The branches above shook so much that a pigeon flew noisily to roost in the next tree, where he continued his purring song undisturbed.

'Can you see anything, Kate? What are they doing?' The anxious voice came from the boy who was leaning against the elm trunk, nervously breaking off pieces of its rough bark.

'There's the cornfield and a corner of the road all white by the bushes, and I think — wait until I have gone up again.' Katharine craned her neck as she sped still higher. 'There are horses, the men look like soldiers — only a few of them coming down the road — and some more coming out of our gates.'

Nicholas sprang forward and seized the ropes of the swing, nearly jolting his sister from her seat. 'Why doesn't he do something?' he demanded fiercely. 'Why doesn't he stop them?'

'Who?' asked Katharine.

'Our father, of course.'

The seven-year-old Katharine regarded her brother wonderingly. 'He may do. You can't fire on people until they are near enough,' she suggested.

'He doesn't intend to fire at all. If he did, you would not be allowed down here to play,' Nicholas replied with calm logic. 'Kate, why aren't you older?'

Katharine was silent, for she could do nothing to overcome that disadvantage. Nicholas was fourteen, and the difference in their ages had meant that they had practically been brought up apart. Katharine, after their mother's death, had been cared for by their cousin Hester. It was the custom for poor orphans, as their cousin was, to go to live with richer relations, being educated and learning household ways at the same time as giving their services. Katharine, at seven, was scarcely out of the nursery, happy with her dolls, sewing, music and simple lessons, whereas Nicholas was struggling with Latin, enjoying fencing, dancing and riding.

Nicholas came early to an understanding of the war which had always seemed a part of their lives. He soon learned that the King, Charles I, and his Parliament were fighting each other for the right to govern the country in the way they thought best, and for the best way to allow the people to worship God. Ceaselessly, year after year, either the Royalists for the King, or the Roundheads—so nicknamed because many of them cropped their hair short—for Parliament, would gain victories, until most of the south and east of the country remained for Parliament and the north and west for the Crown. Torn in between were towns, villages and fortified houses, which one week found themselves belonging to the King, and the next to Parliament, as the battles were fought around them. Even in people's homes the civil war continued when father and sons chose to serve on opposite sides.

In the summer of 1645 the children's father, a Royalist, was in command of the defence of his own walled stronghold in Gloucestershire. Though small, it guarded the main road and was a rallying point of hope to the King's armies near by, who were beginning to foresee their utter defeat in the successes of their enemies. For weeks previously, Nicholas had watched with excitement as the preparations to withstand an attack became more hurried. The news that a force of Roundheads was marching to wipe out pockets of Royalist resistance spread terror through the countryside.

On the day that the womenfolk of the household crowded like frightened sheep into his father's presence, Nicholas watched in scorn and pride. He listened to their pleas and fears. Pleas for a quick surrender, to remember the safety of the children, fears that they would all be murdered in their beds, that the house would be burned over them. When he was ordered curtly from the room, Nicholas went in confidence, sure of his father's leadership, remembering the arms and food laid by, enough for a month's siege.

After two days of inactivity, doubts began to form in the boy's mind. Although the house was ready for attack, an uneasy calm hovered over it. Nicholas was the more uneasy because his small sister was allowed freely into the gardens.

'She will come to some harm if they start firing from a distance,' he thought, and went down to join her at the swing under the elm.

It was there that Katharine announced with childish innocence that she could see their father and one or two others riding out of the main gates to meet the expected enemy. It was then that Nicholas realized that his father had no intention of defending them or the house, but was going to surrender everything, including his honour, for the sake of safety.

'Does it matter so much that he is not going to fight?' Katharine asked, wriggling on the unsteady swing.

'Matter!' Nicholas exclaimed. He crouched at her feet. 'Kate, don't you understand? We are for the King. You cannot be for somebody and then at the first sign of danger give up and run away.'

'Perhaps he is afraid. I should be afraid, I shouldn't want to be killed.'

'Men aren't afraid,' Nicholas said with conviction. 'When you are as old as I am, standing up for what you believe in means more than death. You might be frightened,' he added, seeing his sister's hazel eyes grow round with amazement at this statement, 'but you must never show it. He has given in without a word. Why, Kate? Why has he done it? He is being disloyal to the King, who needs every man he can get. If I had the chance I would serve him myself.'

Katharine went on wriggling until Nicholas in his despondency let the ropes loose, and she was able to work herself up again, up over the wall and the golden cornfield to the two groups of horsemen face to face on the road. The groups merged into one and the double number moved slowly under the gateway.

'They've come in,' she whispered excitedly.

Nicholas paid no attention, but tight-lipped, went on snapping the bark between his fingers.

There was the patter of hurrying footsteps and two of the women servants appeared on the path between the high yew hedges.

'Katharine, child, you should not be here,' one cried on seeing her.

'Poor little one,' the other murmured and tried to gather Kate up in her arms.

Katharine struggled from her grasp. 'I am not afraid,' she protested, although their white faces had nearly dispelled the confidence Nicholas had given her.

They led her away, back to her rooms, where she was surrounded by more women of the household, each working the other up into greater hysteria by suggesting what their fate would be at the hands of the Parliamentarian soldiers.

They need not have feared. They were not murdered in their beds nor the house burned over them. Instead, everyone was treated with courtesy, and it seemed to Katharine, to whom the following days were uneventful, that it made no difference whether the house was held by Royalist or Roundhead. In fact, on the one occasion when she accidentally met her father walking in the gardens with his supposed gaolers, the two men who accompanied him did not behave as she imagined enemies should. One of them took her hand and asked to be shown the swing, and the other willingly pushed her in it when she was seated. But her father leaned against the elm trunk as Nicholas had done, not smiling in his usual manner and not hearing her delighted cries as she flew higher and higher.

As the days passed, Nicholas, whom Katharine normally

saw rarely, spent most of his time in her suite of nursery rooms, avoiding the enemy officers and his father in particular. He sat sullenly through her lessons, not listening or reading but staring out of the window. Katharine gradually became sensitive to the varying atmospheres around her, especially among the women when Cousin Hester tried to stem their chatter for fear that the child would pick up gossip not fit for her ears. Katharine, although pretending to be engrossed in embroidery or learning passages from the Bible, listened, thrilled and fearful, to the tales of further fighting. The Royalists had won a victory and the Roundheads were retreating, withdrawing their troops from village and house. The women whispered again of the treatment they might receive in revenge as the soldiers were forced to leave their stronghold, and although Katharine could not imagine the two officers who had played with her wanting to harm any of them, she grew more nervous, too.

On the morning that the Roundheads were due to leave, Katharine escaped from Cousin Hester to the safety of the swing under the elm. There she felt secure in a world of her own, the dark yews behind, thick branches above, the castellated wall in front and nothing but air under her feet as she swung in the sunshine. Nicholas joined her, and together they watched the orderly departure of the troopers as they had watched their arrival. With as little ceremony as possible the Roundheads rode away, not a shot having been fired nor a living creature harmed.

'I wonder why they came,' Katharine remarked, as the column rounded the bend in the road. 'It cannot have made much difference to them, just holding a house and a village, and it has made no difference to us, has it?' she asked her brother.

He did not reply, and when his fingers touched Katharine's as he pushed the swing, she noticed they were icy cold.

'Will the King come, now?' she asked.

'Not himself — Royalist soldiers,' was the impatient answer.

'And will they be as kind as the others who played with me?'

'If you keep looking over the wall you may see them, they were in the village last night.' His voice was sharp, for his sister's prattle irritated him when his whole body was on edge with anxiety. How were the now victorious Royalists going to greet the man who had given his trust so willingly into enemy hands? Why had he done it? Was his father a traitor or a coward, or were there deep political reasons which the Royalists would understand? Until that strange decision Nicholas had held his father in admiration and respect. He was young, easy-tempered, sport-loving, seemingly more interested in his dogs and horses than the fluctuating battles, and reading his Bible at family prayers with a liveliness which would have shocked many of his more serious neighbours.

Katharine swung happily, working herself up, grasping the rope with one hand and her fluttering skirt with the other, secretly delighted when her petticoats refused to be held down and she could see the gaily-coloured garters, which she had made herself, gripping the stockings above her knees. The bright buckles on her shoes caught the light and threw sparks of sunshine into the shadows, until one spark seemed to fly hovering beyond the poppies at the edge of the road to become instead a patch of gold on a man's chest.

'Soldiers!' she exclaimed. 'It must be the King's men. There are more than there were of the others and one of them has a big banner. Please, Nick,' she scraped her feet along the ground to slacken the swing's speed, 'please, may we go and watch them?'

Nicholas lifted her down, and again his cold fingers closed over her warm ones as he took her hand to check her eager run to the yew hedge. This time there were no hurrying footsteps to urge her indoors, and she walked quietly at his side, not daring to speak or ask questions after she had glanced at the tense face above her. He led her to the black yew archway which framed the whole of the court in front of the house.

After the shade and grass under the elm tree, the heat of the summer noon quivered from the burning stones, the women who had come out to greet their liberators glowed like clusters of flowers on the terrace. Katharine gazed in awe at the silent men, grouped before her like people in a painting with neat black shadows beneath each figure. It seemed to her, that it should have been a scene of rejoicing with everyone laughing and happy because the Roundheads had gone away. Instead, there was a heavy stillness and she could feel her brother's arm trembling against her shoulder.

As she waited, the picture came to life. A tall man stepped from his group and approached her father, who was standing alone at the foot of the terrace; he moved forward and they began to speak. Katharine heard the words 'surrender to the enemy' and 'traitor'. She looked quickly up at Nicholas, who was crushing her fingers between his until they hurt.

'Are they angry?' she whispered. 'Are they angry because he let the Roundheads come in? What will they do to him, Nick?' Her voice was thin with fear.

'They might hang him.' The four words dropped like slivers of ice through the hot afternoon.

Katharine pushed the knuckles of her free hand between her teeth. Then she saw her father slip to his knees, holding out his arms as if in supplication, while his little jet shadow mimicked and mocked his movements.

'Why is he doing that?' she asked, although she really knew.

'He is asking them to spare his life.' The reply was full of bitter disillusionment. Nicholas wrenched his fingers from her grasp. 'Has he no courage, no pride?' he muttered. 'Why cannot someone stop him degrading himself any more?'

Katharine sensed his horror and his shame, and his shattered world. Like a blue butterfly she darted past him, across the yellow stones to clutch her father's shoulder.

'Stop, stop,' she cried. 'You mustn't.'

Overbalanced by her unexpected assault, he fell sideways

and they both tumbled to the ground. Katharine burst into tears at the sight of his wan, startled face.

The soldiers thought she did not want them to harm her father, not that her cry was to him to save what dignity he had left. The man nearest to her caught her up in his arms. Through her tears she saw blue eyes, a kind smile and a white lace collar which she clung to gratefully. The officer carried her to the women on the terrace.

'You should have better care of the child than this,' he said sharply. 'Take her indoors and keep yourselves at the back of the house.'

Hester, more afraid of him than she had been of the Parliamentarians, clasped Katharine to her and beckoned the other women to follow inside.

For hours, it seemed to Katharine, she was nursed and petted. Her doll was pushed into her hands, sweetmeats were pushed into her mouth. She was told repeatedly that there was nothing to be afraid of. She suffered their embraces and fondling arms in stolid silence, not seeing the swirling skirts around her, but only her father, once so magnificent in shining breastplate and helmet on his great brown horse, grovelling on the dirty stones of the forecourt.

She shared her brother's shame, and when he came into the room, dressed for travelling, sword at his side, hat in hand, she went eagerly to meet him.

'I am leaving, Kate, to serve the King,' he said.

There was no warmth in his voice. The years between them suddenly seemed many more, and he was no longer the older brother who would push her on the swing and hear her baby lessons. Nicholas looked at Katharine. Her impulsive action had only added to his humiliation and he did not see before him a sister who had tried to help, but a small girl, large-eyed, her face sticky with comfits, a wooden doll pressed against the grubby bodice of her dress.

'Father?' she whispered, knowing it was a stupid question for she guessed the answer.

'Your father is dead,' Nicholas replied. 'They gave him the honour of being shot.'

A low moan from the women greeted his words. 'God be thanked she is too young to understand,' Hester murmured.

Katharine's fingers tightened on her doll. They never thought she understood anything.

Nicholas bent quickly and kissed her forehead. 'God be with you, Kate, I shall not come back.'

Katharine watched him, misery welling up inside her, as he left the room. She had tried to bridge the gap between them and failed; she had said 'Good-bye' with a mouth sticky like a baby's, and what was worse she had shown she was still a baby by saying that the coming of the Roundheads had made no difference, but Nicholas had known that the world could never be the same again.

Chapter II

Fugitives from the Battle

IT was the feeling that he was lying in a pool of water, that awoke Matthew. He opened his eyes slowly and sat up. His body had made a shallow hollow in the already damp undergrowth and rain was still dripping from the overhanging trees, seeping through his clothes, making them cling to his wet skin. He shifted his position, and glanced across in the darkness to where the broad shape of his brother leaned away from the tree trunk, avoiding the trickles which ran down the bark. He was sitting in exactly the same way as when Matthew had last looked at him before falling asleep, arms on knees, hat on the back of his head, alert, and finishing the remains of a stolen apple. Apples, apples and blackberries. Matthew's stomach turned over at the thought. He had lived on nothing but those for the past few days, with an occasional slice of bread and an egg from a friendly, but cautious, villager, who had tried not to recognize the two dishevelled young men and boy for what he knew them to be—fugitives from the recently fought battle at Worcester.

Matthew's stirrings caused his brother to turn his head. 'Rested?' he queried.

'I am soaked through,' the boy replied.

'So am I, but we should be able to move soon. It has been dark for some time and I have heard nothing.'

'Is Nick still asleep?' Matthew asked.

The recumbent figure on the far side of his brother showed signs of life, and a muffled voice, from under the hat which had been placed over its face to shield it from the rain, mumbled an answer.

'Nick is awake and has been for an hour,' it said.

Nicholas sat up, shaking the water from the brim of the hat before replacing it on his head. 'Brr——' he muttered. 'What a country to be an outlaw in! It must be the wettest place on earth. At least this week can go down in history as the most depressing I have ever known—no—one of the most,' he corrected himself. 'And let it be told to all succeeding generations,' he went on with mock jocularity, 'that on the third of September, in the year of our Lord sixteen hundred and fifty-one, the King's cause and the Royalist hope suffered its most crushing defeat at the battle of Worcester. Here are we, stragglers from that vain hope, afraid for our lives, hiding like common criminals from our own countrymen, who would readily string us up like so many strangled chickens from the nearest tree.'

The bitterness underlying his tone was obvious, and Matthew hesitated to ask the question that was uppermost in his mind.

'What about the King?' he faltered hoarsely; the damp seemed to have crept into his throat too.

'Heaven help him, for there are few here who will do so,' was the low reply.

Matthew said no more, afraid to interrupt the thoughts of his companions who, after this remark, had fallen into a brooding gloom.

For all Matthew's life the country had been torn by civil war, which had not ended with the execution of Charles I in 1649. Matthew's father, a Royalist, his estates forfeited to Parliament, had fled abroad with his wife and elder son, Giles. Matthew, only a small boy at the time, had been left in the care of an uncle until it would be possible for him to join his parents. But two years later, when the new King, Charles II, had landed in Scotland to try to regain his throne, Giles and many other exiled Cavaliers had accompanied him. On the march into England, through Shropshire, where Matthew was living, the two brothers were reunited. Matthew was taken from what he felt was a dull life and thrown into the excitement of army existence with his brother and his brother's friend Nicholas. Nicholas was an enigma to them both. Giles had met him in Holland, deep in the intrigue for restoring the young King to his kingdom, one of the first to leap into danger when they landed, lively and good-humoured; yet they knew nothing about him. He never mentioned his family or where he had lived in England before his exile, and even his name, Nicholas Trent, they sometimes felt was not his own. But, Giles had told his young brother firmly, if Nicholas wished to keep his past life private that was no concern of theirs.

Matthew cast his mind back over the last weeks. They had marched so hopefully, if wearily, to Worcester, there to be attacked by Oliver Cromwell's iron-clad, disciplined troops. After a fierce battle, which had raged until dusk, the Royalist ranks were broken and in flight. Charles and some of his loyal supporters, determined not to let him suffer the same fate as his father, galloped from the north gate of the town hoping to hide in the Welsh mountains until he could be safely shipped to France. Unfortunately, Oliver Cromwell had been a step ahead of most ideas. He soon had roads, bridges and ports guarded, as Giles and Nicholas had quickly discovered. There were troopers, and even ordinary villagers, on the look out for any strangers who might be Royalists in disguise. That was why the three of them were now lying in the damp woods on a September evening, not daring to move until darkness fell.

To get as far away from Worcester as they could, had been their first idea, but, as Giles sat watching while his brother and Nicholas slept, he wondered how long it would be possible for them to remain hidden. How many miles was it to the nearest coast where they might get a boat for the Continent? Where was the money coming from to pay the master of a vessel, and bribe him into believing some invented story? How were they to get food without arousing suspicions? He had promised his parents that if the King's venture were unsuccessful he would somehow take Matthew back to France with him, and that was a promise he fully intended to keep.

Nicholas broke the silence by pulling his hat over his ears and struggling to his feet.

'We had better go,' he said.

'Where?' Giles asked. 'Isn't it time that we made some plans?'

'To-night,' Nicholas replied cheerfully, 'I intend to sleep between sheets on a feather mattress in my own home.'

'Your home?' Matthew exclaimed, momentarily forgetting his tiredness in his excitement.

Giles could not help smiling. For the last few days Nicholas, although suffering from a sword cut in his foot, which had swollen painfully with the hard walking, had insisted on leading them, and had accepted without comment their admiration for his guidance across rough country. Naturally, if he had grown up in the area, Giles thought with amusement, that was why he knew it so well.

When they were ready, Matthew took his place in the middle of the single file with more hopefulness than he had felt for some hours. He had not dared to complain of his weariness, nor of his blistered heels and toes rubbed into sores by the wet leather of his boots. Giles and Nicholas were in danger and he was not going to damage their chances of escape because he was the youngest and weakest.

He lost count of time and distance as he stumbled along behind Nicholas's limping figure, and if he lost ground, a prod from his brother urged him on. At last, when Nicholas stopped at the bottom of a copse which bordered a road glistening with puddles in the starlight, Matthew dropped down where he was and let the whispered conversation of the other two drift over him. As he was lying with his head close to the ground his ear caught the vibration and regular thudding of approaching hoof-beats.

'Horses!' he hissed, sitting up alert and watchful.

For a moment neither of them believed him.

'Down in the ditch,' Nicholas muttered, as the sounds became unmistakable.

He rolled by Matthew's side, noisily crackling twigs as he tried to lie comfortably. Giles crouched behind them, his head slightly raised, his breathing quick and light. Matthew sensed that he was calmly calculating the distance between them and the soldiers, and their chances of escaping notice. They were Cromwellian troopers and only Giles saw them pass. Both Nicholas and Matthew, with the same idea that their staring eyes would attract the men's attention, kept their faces hidden in their arms.

'I only hope they are not sharing the hospitality of my home,' Nicholas murmured, when a shake from Giles told him it was safe to sit up.

'Are we close?' Giles asked.

'Across the road and down a lane on the right. We will not risk the main gate, but come up through the garden at the back. There used to be a gate in the wall.'

Nicholas wriggled out of the ditch. Matthew tried to follow him, but for once his legs refused to obey. They were limp with exhaustion.

'Carry him,' Nicholas suggested, as Giles slipped his hands under the boy's shoulders to lift him up.

In spite of protests Matthew was hoisted on to his brother's back. They crossed the road, found the lane, which showed signs of frequent use, and skirted a high wall. Nicholas went carefully, groping along the stones, feeling for the familiar gap with its narrow, iron gateway. At length, his fingers touched the metal latch, which he raised, and putting his shoulder against the framework he pushed hard. The gate flew open, dragging him with it across the muddy path.

'They keep the back entrance in better repair than when I lived here,' he whispered, steadying himself against the wall.

'Is it so long ago?' Giles asked.

'Six years,' was the quick reply. 'I suppose a good deal

can happen in six years and I ought to be prepared for change.'

Giles waited silently for his friend to move forward. In the space of an hour he had learnt more about Nicholas than in a whole year's acquaintance; the position of his home, that it was prosperous, or had been, and that Nicholas had left it at fourteen, an early age to come away alone without a very good reason. He closed the gate with his foot and followed through a clearing containing one large tree, and on to a path between thick, uncut hedges to an archway leading to a paved court. The only sounds were the patterings of rain from the dripping leaves, and Matthew's heavy breathing because his head had lolled in sleep across his brother's neck. Nicholas was standing staring into the darkness, and for a moment Giles was afraid there must be some unseen danger.

'That is a change I had not expected.' Nicholas's words were scarcely above a whisper, but they were immediately understood. In front, rose the black mass of a house; its roof, jagged and bare against the lighter sky, showed that it was in ruins.

Giles sensed the feeling of shock and bitterness. 'We may find shelter in a barn just for the night,' he suggested gently.

'Someone will be living here, in the lodge most likely. Follow me.' Nicholas spoke sharply and his actions were the same. He seemed to have forgotten that they were fugitives, and limped with little caution across the yard, his feet striking angrily against the broken stones.

As there was a light showing between the shutters of the lodge windows, he thumped unhesitatingly upon the door under the low porch. Giles drew back, watching carefully, and shifted his inert brother into his arms where he could be more easily slipped to the ground. After a long pause the door was opened, and through the crack appeared a candle and a woman's face.

'Cousin Hester?' Nicholas asked.

The door swung wide, the woman's hand flew to her mouth

to check the scream as she saw the man standing there, with the powerful figure of Giles behind him.

'Nicholas,' she whispered. 'Nicholas.'

'May I come into my own home?' he asked, as she still barred the way.

She stepped aside to let them pass and, as they entered, they both looked across the room to the hearth. Opposite them, clasping an armful of wood to the bodice of her shabby white dress, stood a young girl. She was slight, pale, freckled, with fair hair, parted like a boy's, falling down each side of her face. Katharine had been a plump seven-year-old, and the six years had made an even greater change in her. She was thin, Nicholas thought, and as her eyes met his he was swept back to that day when she had said good-bye with a sticky mouth and a doll pressed to her chest. It was a reminder of the day he had spent years trying to forget, in building a new name for himself and a character as alien to his father's as was possible.

The girl suddenly dropped the wood and ran to greet him.

'Nick!' she cried. 'Nick! And you said you would never come back.'

That, again, was an unfortunate reminder, and Nicholas pushed the embracing arms gently away. 'Circumstances have forced my hand, Katharine,' he said.

Giles saw that she was hurt. 'May my brother rest here?' he asked quickly, indicating the long, padded settle in front of the fire. 'He is worn out; we have been hiding and walking for days.'

The girl nodded and bent to pick up her pieces of wood. The noise had awakened Matthew, who, on seeing where he was, and in the company of two women, went scarlet with shame and indignation at Giles for allowing him to remain asleep. He swung his legs from the seat, propped his elbows on his knees and stared sullenly at the floor. Nicholas hobbled to a chair, drew a knife and began cutting the boot from his swollen foot.

Giles turned to the woman who had been addressed as Cousin Hester. She had fastened the door and had drawn thick curtains to cover the chinks in the shutters. She, too, had a pale, oval face, but with dark, greying hair. He smiled, and, feeling the faint air of embarrassment, took it upon himself to explain where they had come from and who he and Matthew were. He was annoyed with Nicholas for behaving so rudely. It was only natural that he should be upset on finding his home in ruins, although after six years the position could have been worse, but there was no need to be so abrupt with a younger sister who was delighted to see him.

Cousin Hester went to the fire to fetch warm water and cloths for them to bathe their feet. 'You will be safe here for a while,' she said. 'The soldiers have not troubled us as yet.'

'That is not surprising.' Nicholas spoke curtly. He eased the boot painfully from his leg, and Giles knelt to help him. 'How long,' he went on, 'has the place been like this?'

'Why, since you left.' Hester showed her amazement at his ignorance. 'Did you expect them to leave it standing after——'

'And you have lived in the lodge?' Nicholas interrupted.

'Katharine and I, and a few servants. Some of the men, Bailey the steward, and his wife live over the stables. We have tried to keep a home for you, Nicholas.' Her voice was quiet and a little reproachful at his hard manner.

Giles went on bathing and bandaging his friend's foot, trying to be as unobtrusive as possible because he guessed there must be a great deal they wanted to say to each other, but doubting that Nicholas would be very frank after his first forceful interruption.

'Most of the grounds are overgrown,' Hester continued. 'We have our own vegetables and fruit, the cows and the hens. It has not been easy, and the most difficult of all has been to see that Katharine was brought up in a way your parents would have wished. I have done all I could, but it is very quiet here now, sheltered and lonely.'

Nicholas looked from his cousin to his sister, who was ladling broth from a cauldron on the fire into pewter bowls. After the spontaneous pleasure of her welcome and his rebuff, she had shrunk inside herself. She seemed shy, frightened, unused to male company, and blushed violently whenever the newcomers' eyes strayed in her direction.

When he had finished helping Nicholas, Giles went deliberately to the hearth to take the bowls, for he hoped that a word of kindness and explanation might ease the girl's misery.

'Katharine,' he began, and almost wished he had not spoken because her neck and cheeks burned with sudden colour. 'We are ill-mannered and tired. In the morning we may have come to our senses.'

She understood his meaning because she smiled. 'It is different for Nicholas,' she murmured. 'He has been away and done exciting things, while I have been here and everything has been the same — nearly the same — not the same as before he left. I wondered where he was and imagined all the brave things he was doing, because he would be brave, wouldn't he?' She raised her eyes anxiously as though the answer mattered desperately.

'Always,' Giles replied, puzzled by her concern.

'There wasn't anything else to think about except him. But Nicholas has been busy — and sisters do not mean much to their elder brothers, especially when they are not very pleased with them. It — it all happened after my fa——'

He had to stop her from going on. If she was about to tell him what Nicholas had never divulged, he would have to destroy her new-found confidence. 'I know nothing about your brother, his home or you,' he broke in as gently as possible.

Even her fingertips flamed with her confusion and pain, so that Giles took the bowls quickly and passed them to Nicholas and Matthew. It was a relief when, at that moment, Hester called the child from the room to help prepare the beds upstairs.

Nicholas stirred his broth thoughtfully, and his eyes glanced over the familiar objects of the lodge kitchen.

'I used to come here when I wanted to play truant from my tutor,' he said. 'It was dirty and smelled of grease and candles, dogs and cooking, but I loved it, because it was a haven from everything that was tidy and proper in a boy's life.' He paused. 'I never thought the day would come when I should hate the sight of it.'

Again, Giles was silent, hoping his friend would say more, and so explain his harshness towards his sister and his bitterness on revisiting his home. But Nicholas was silent, too, deep in gloomy thoughts.

When Hester returned, without Katharine, who had gone to bed, it was she and Giles who maintained a thread of conversation, until the meal was finished and the more definite topic of their escape was discussed.

Chapter III

A Plan for Escape

WHEN he awoke in the morning, Matthew lay contentedly in the narrow truckle bed at the foot of the large four-poster, where his brother and Nicholas had slept. He stretched his toes with relief and happiness that he was no longer lying in a ditch or hollow of wet leaves. His muscles ached, but it was a comfortable ache, wrapped round with the warm blankets and the knowledge that he would not have to spring up at a moment's notice to begin another weary day. For the first time since he had joined Giles, he longed for the security of a home again, food, clean clothes, the routine of lessons and a sight of the falcon his uncle had given him. He hoped that it would be possible for them to remain in Nicholas's home for some days. Although he had paid little attention to the woman, Mistress Hester, he had liked her. She had not treated him as a child, probably because he was tall and looked older than his age; she had not suggested that he should be put to bed, when his brother and Nicholas had stayed talking in the dark kitchen late into the night and he had nodded continually because he was so tired. The person he disliked was the insipid girl, Katharine. She was so different from her brother, and Matthew could not help thinking that if she had not been there, Nicholas would not have changed into the moody, irritable fellow he had become. Her presence had spoiled a very pleasant friendship. She was weak and he admired strength, and he was jealous of the fact that Giles, with a natural love of anything helpless—animal or child—had gone out of his way to be kind to her.

Matthew yawned, and seeing that the large bed was empty, reluctantly pushed his sheets away and hobbled across to the table on which stood a bowl and copper jug of water. He shivered as he dipped in his fingers, for the water was cold, which showed that the other two must have been up and dressed for some time. He washed, although the ball of soap scarcely lathered, and put on his own soiled suit, and pulled the stiff leather boots over his still painful feet.

On the way downstairs he came face to face with the girl, Katharine. She smiled shyly, a slow smile which spread from her eyes to her lips.

'There is food for you in the kitchen,' she said, and went back with him. 'We laid it in the kitchen in case anyone saw you—anyone outside,' she explained hastily, her cheeks flaming at his steady gaze. 'All our servants are loyal and would do anything to help you.'

'When did my brother come down?' Matthew asked. He spoke abruptly, partly because he felt awkward in her company and partly because he was annoyed that Giles had gone without waking him.

'An hour ago. They went to the stables with Bailey—he is our steward—to see about horses if they needed them. They thought it might be safe to stay a few more nights and then leave on horseback, because Nicholas cannot walk far with his foot. It is not going to be easy for you,' she added sympathetically.

Matthew sat down at the table. He did not want her sympathy and he was irritated that she knew more of their plans than he did. 'You need have no fears about us,' he said with condescension. 'We have outwitted these Roundheads before and they cannot recognize a Royalist when they see one. Why, at an inn we stopped at a day or two ago, there were soldiers in the yard and Giles had to pretend to be an ostler, and he heard all about the battle, and rumours of the King, too. Giles is like the King in height and colouring, but they did not recognize him—most of them have never seen the King, or met anyone who has. They have not the wits or the brains to do us much harm,' he said, quoting from snatches of idle camp gossip.

'They seem to have been successful so far,' the girl replied with unexpected heat, goaded by his superior tone. 'They have won the war. Why did not the King win if all his followers were so witty and clever? I can tell you,' she went on swiftly, taking advantage of Matthew's full mouth, and quoting from their own servants' chatter. 'Because they were always quarrelling among themselves as to who should be the leader of the armies, and the King — the old King — said one thing and did another. No one could believe or trust a word he said, and Queen Henrietta interfered. She was a Roman Catholic and no one trusts Catholics after Queen Mary. My Cousin Hester is a Catholic but it is not the same, she is not powerful like the Queen. Women should not meddle in politics, they can think what they like, but they should not meddle. King Charles wanted to make out that he was fulfilling God's will on earth, the divine right of Kings he called it, but it wasn't, it was just what he wanted to do himself.'

'King Charles I was a martyr and died for his beliefs,' Matthew interrupted fiercely. 'His trial was no trial, he was murdered by rebels. You speak as though you agree with Oliver Cromwell and Parliament; no wonder your brother was not pleased to see you. I should not have thought you had much to thank the Roundheads for — they burned your home and killed your father, surely?'

'No, they did not,' Katharine flashed, nearly in tears. 'I wish they had.' She picked up a basket from the end of the table and fled from the room.

Astounded at her reply, Matthew watched her go with relief. He hurriedly finished his meal and went across to the stables, where he was told that his brother was mending harness under the elm by the far wall. The path took him between the yew hedges and into the clearing that he had been too sleepy to notice the night before.

Giles and Nicholas were kneeling in the grass rubbing mildewed leathers and rusted buckles, which had been allowed to fall into poor condition through lack of use. In answer to Matthew's enquiry as to why they were there and not in the yard, Giles replied that it was safer.

'If any troopers come to the house and want stabling for horses, it will not be easy to deceive them if there is a heap of newly polished harness on the floor. It can be hidden here and we can have a better warning of their approach.'

'Do you think they will come?' Matthew asked.

'We saw a party last night on the road and Bailey has had news already this morning that they are in the village searching for fugitives or the King. I don't think it will be long before the house and grounds are ransacked.'

'But—but in that case, wouldn't it be better if we left now?' Matthew suggested, not able to see the reason for waiting to be caught.

'We are safer where we are,' Nicholas told him again. 'We need the horses and no one will betray us. If you climb on to the top of the wall, you should be able to see the road they will use and tell us when they appear on the bend.'

Although for once doubting their wisdom, and certainly not sharing their unruffled manner, Matthew obeyed. His toes dug into the cracks between the stones, and he pulled himself up until he was able to sit in one of the deep embrasures and gaze across the countryside. It was a dreary green world that met his eyes, for bindweed, brambles, clusters of ripe elderberries fought with each other for a footing beneath him. Beyond, were broken pergolas on which jasmine and roses had been trained, the paved forecourt with long, brown tufts of grass pushing up the flags, and black puddles of rainwater in the hollows, the ruined gateway and the rough track curving round the edge of a ploughed field. He watched for some minutes, not expecting to see any movement on the deserted road, and when, at length, a thin line of horsemen drew into sight he could not believe that they were real. He glanced doubtfully at Giles and Nicholas busy on the ground, and back at the riders, who had grown a little larger and a little more distinct.

'There are some horsemen — they may be troopers,' he whispered.

Nicholas dropped his work and climbed up beside him. 'Yes,' he muttered, giving them the quickest of looks.

Before he could slip down again, there was the sound of heavy footsteps running along the path towards them and into the clearing came Bailey, dragging by the hand a breathless Katharine.

'You have never seen either of them, your brother or Giles, if they ask,' he was saying. 'You have been picking fruit and sent to find the boy, Matthew, who is wanted to chop wood. Is that clear?'

Katharine nodded. She was almost as white as her dress. In her hands she was clutching the basket, now full of apples and pears.

'Matthew,' the steward went on, 'stay on the wall. Don't speak much, touch your forelock if they ask too many questions and smile and shake your head. You two' — he turned to Giles and Nicholas, who had waited, knowing their lives depended on the man's speed and knowledge — 'up the tree as high as you can. If we get out of this we must find you a better disguise; you are too respectable by far. Leave the leathers, I'll take those.'

Giles handed his straps to the steward and gave Nicholas a hoist into the lower branches before climbing up himself. For an anxious moment the elm shook, the boughs quivered under the extra weight and showers of tiny leaves, some green, some yellow, were scattered into the long grass.

'It's a mercy there's no birds,' Bailey muttered. 'They would have given us away. I'll fetch you myself later,' he added, and, gathering the saddles in his arms, staggered off through the undergrowth.

Silence fell over the clearing. Katharine stood perfectly still, gripping the basket in both hands. She was living the past again, for in her imagination she could see the soldiers dismounting in the forecourt, orderly and disciplined, unhurried as before. 'Soon,' she thought, 'someone will come down the path to fetch me and it will happen all over again.' She heard the footsteps and the swish of the uncut grass as it was brushed aside, but, as the Cromwellian soldier entered the clearing, the basket slipped from her fingers and she

crumpled to the ground. Leaves fluttered from above to pattern her white dress.

Matthew slithered from the wall and stood staring from Katharine to the naked sword, which slashed the stinging-nettles between him and the soldier.

'Don't just look at her, boy, come and pick up some of this fruit,' shouted the trooper.

Matthew moved cautiously. 'W-what are you going to do?' he asked, as the man bent over Katharine.

'What do you think? Eat her?' he asked. 'First it is Prince Rupert who is the monster and the mothers keep their children quiet with tales of his wickedness. Now, it is Oliver Cromwell who is the terror of the land and treated like a fire-eating dragon of old. You country folk are as changeable as weathercocks. Fill the basket and tell me where the child comes from. Then I will take her back.'

'From the lodge,' Matthew muttered, hoping he would be left alone.

The trooper, who had sheathed his sword, lifted Katharine up into his arms and waited until the basket was almost full. Then, with a curt nod for Matthew to lead the way, he strode from the clearing.

After that, the hours for Matthew became confused. There was Mistress Hester, her skirts looped up and her scarlet petticoats swinging round her ankles as she ran to meet them. There was Bailey, giving him a cuff on the ear and telling him to be off to the wood-yard; and there were the soldiers, whom he saw out of the corner of his eye as he chopped wood, searching through the ruins, running swords through bales of straw and pitchforks into ricks to see if any fugitives were concealed there. Finally, after the men had mounted and clattered under the archway on to the road, when the dull sky cleared at last and a pale lemon light shone over the horizon, Matthew limped wearily indoors. He hoped for some praise for his uncomplaining hours of heavy work.

Katharine was resting on the settle, Giles was at her side, and in another chair, slumped in front of the fire, sat Nicholas. A day spent in the cramped branches of the elm tree had not improved his moodiness. Matthew's excitement and desire to talk quickly died, especially when Hester, who was hurriedly preparing the meal she had not dared to touch earlier, asked him to baste the meat.

'Girl's work,' Matthew thought in annoyance as he passed Katharine to crouch on the floor in front of the spit. It revolved slowly, the rich brown juice trickling over the dark meat as he scooped it from the trough below. 'She ought to have recovered by now, it was hours ago that she fainted.'

Hester placed loaves and butter on the table. 'It is plain enough after to-day that you cannot stay here much longer,' she murmured.

'Most of the harness is ready and Bailey says he can find us the horses,' Nicholas replied.

'But where are we to go?' Giles asked. 'Can the three of us ride as we are through any town or village to the sea? What story are we to tell if questioned?'

No one answered, until Katharine, half afraid to disturb their silence, broke in unexpectedly. 'I remember once, Hester,' she began, 'that you went to visit a relation of yours — because she was having a baby and needed help. Couldn't you go to visit your cousin Sarah Barfutt in Hampshire?'

Nicholas looked at his sister as if he thought her fainting attack had affected her more seriously than he had imagined, and Hester snapped impatiently.

'What are you talking about, child?' she asked. 'Cousin Barfutt is too old for bearing children and she has been a widow these ten years. What has that to do with your brother's escape, I should like to know?'

'I only thought,' Katharine replied meekly, scarlet at the rebuke, 'that your cousin lived in the New Forest, and the Forest is near the sea, and as France is only the other side of the sea——' she stopped, embarrassed by the interest she had aroused and the unwavering eyes fixed on her face.

'My Cousin Barfutt,' Hester repeated, as she understood her meaning. Her mind went back over the years, to the months after she had lost both her parents and had gone to live in the Forest with her cousin Sarah. Sarah was a year or two older, so strong and determined that Hester looked up to her as an elder sister, admiring her capable handling of her father's animals, and envying her the farm which would one day be hers on Master Virgin's death. Then the letter had arrived from Hester's distant relations in the north, asking if she would make her home with them as nurse and companion for the new baby, Katharine. 'She would help us, I know,' she said out loud. 'The farm is no more than a few miles from the sea near Christchurch, and she might know of someone who owned a boat and could get you out of the country.'

'There is the journey to the farm to be made first,' Nicholas muttered.

'I know what Katharine thinks we could do,' Giles said, ignoring his friend's despondency. 'Mistress Hester must travel to visit her cousin on some pretext and we could go as her servants.'

'Hester is of the old faith, she is a Roman Catholic,' Nicholas interrupted again. 'She would need a pass from the authorities to say why she was going and how long she intended to stay. They would never allow three servants, two men and a boy, for one woman.'

'Could not Katharine go too?' Matthew suggested quietly, patting the meat and keeping his head averted. Not that he relished her company, but on a long ride on horseback there would be little opportunity for her to affect their spirits if she were mistress and they the servants. 'If she could pretend to be ill and have to travel in a litter, then you would need two horsemen to carry the litter and someone for Mistress Hester to ride pillion with. The soldiers knew she fainted today and would not be surprised if it was said that she was to be taken away in case she was frightened again. She has already been ill once and it should not be difficult for her to pretend a little longer.'

The faint sarcasm was not lost upon Giles, who regarded his brother's back curiously. 'If it can be done, it is our best solution,' he agreed. 'But there are grave risks for your cousin Hester, Nicholas, which we can hardly expect her to take for complete strangers, and risks for Katharine if we are discovered.'

Hester shook her head. In spite of the dangers it would be a change from the monotonous life which she and Katharine led; she would be only too pleased to see her cousin again, and the journey would hold few risks for Katharine, who would only have to lie still and look tired. Nicholas, now that there was some definite plan to work on, immediately showed a lively interest and hobbled to the door, saying that Bailey would be able to help in obtaining Hester's pass, and as there was the problem of the litter to be discussed he ought to come in while they were eating.

Matthew, not daring to meet his brother's accusing eyes, went on basting the meat. He dared not meet Katharine's either, for he knew that she thought he had deliberately suggested her part in the journey because of her rash talk in the kitchen that morning. Then, he had charged her with defending the Roundheads, and this would be her opportunity to show her loyalty to the King and to her brother. She was keeping as still as a mouse on the settle, as if almost wishing that she had not spoken of her idea, and was already fearful of the approaching journey.

Chapter IV

Virgin Farm

IF Matthew had felt when they reached Nicholas's home that, after fleeing from the battle, all he wanted was a comfortable bed, regular meals and peace, he had changed his mind by the time preparations for a second flight were complete. His excitement rose as the litter, a light wooden structure with leather curtains over the open windows, was carefully repaired in the stable after dark. He saw the pass, which Bailey had not found easy to obtain because it had had to be signed by four Justices of the Peace, enabling Hester to travel to Virgin Farm, near Christchurch in Hampshire, and to remain there for two months, so long as in the mean time 'she act nothing to the prejudice of the State'. A sentence which none of them dared linger on for any length of time. Their clothes, which again the steward had provided, from among those of the other servants, to help them in their disguise, were coarse and plain. Both Giles and Nicholas, with their hair trimmed shorter and wearing tall hats, looked like a pair of sober Puritans escorting their mistress on an uninteresting journey.

Instead of the cloudiness which had become usual, the morning of their departure broke upon them with renewed summer brilliance. The September sun was hot, scarcely a leaf was showing the yellow of autumn, and even the puddles in the forecourt lay like blue platters under the clear sky. Matthew harnessed the horses into the shafts of the litter and mounted at the rear. Nicholas was to ride in front, and Giles, with Hester behind him, would be on the third animal. In order to avert any suspicions in case the Roundheads made an unexpected return to the house, Katharine's role as the sick child had to begin at once. Wrapped in a shawl, she was carried by Giles and placed on the rugs and cushions in the litter; the leather curtains were dropped, shutting out all but a narrow streak of daylight at the edges. Hester, her dress covered by a light gown to protect it from the dirt of the roads, was assisted from the mounting-block to her seat behind the saddle, and Nicholas, still finding walking difficult, was glad of a helping hand from the steward.

'If anyone wants to know how you came by that wound, Master Nicholas,' remarked Bailey, 'tell them it was a pitch-fork during harvest.'

Nicholas nodded. He pressed the man's hand affectionately and thanked him for all he had done. He made no elaborate farewells, although he knew it was probably the last time he would see his old home. Now that there was no hope of a king on the throne and the country would be ruled by a common-wealth, the estate could be sold to raise money for his life abroad, if he reached the Continent in safety; it would also provide for the loyal servants and allow Hester and Katharine to live somewhere in reasonable comfort.

The little party moved slowly out of the forecourt, under the ruined arch and on to the road. Nicholas had a good knowledge of the countryside, which made the way easy for some miles. He avoided the villages where possible and the low ground, because after the wet summer the deep lanes were impassable for the swaying litter. He took lonely forest paths and the drovers' tracks across the open moorland.

It was in a sheltered hollow of the heath that they made their first halt of the day. When Matthew had unharnessed the horses and let them loose to graze he returned to find Hester unpacking the hamper of food she had prepared, and Katharine, eyes closed, huddled miserably against a tree trunk. As Giles and Nicholas were resting a few feet away on the grass, Matthew followed their example and lay on his back listening to their subdued conversation as he had so often done before. The battle and days in the ruined house had been depressing, but now, as he crumbled the heather-bells between his fingers, he felt dreamily content. Above the curving birch branches, a lark sang in the height of the sky; there was the bruised scent of the bracken beneath him, and over his head a trail of ripe blackberries heavy with fruit hung motionless in the still air. Matthew smiled, for he no longer hated the sight of blackberries. They almost seemed a happy symbol that no one need starve in England in late summer. Gradually, he became conscious that Katharine's lighter voice had joined in the deep murmurings.

'I cannot eat anything, Nicholas,' she was saying. 'The litter has made me sick. It jolts and sways with every step the horses take. If it had not been for Matthew's idea you would never have made me do it.'

Matthew turned on his side and listened with interest.

'You cannot blame Matthew, Kate,' Nicholas was trying to be patient. 'The three of us had to get away and someone had to be ill in order to account for that number of servants. If you are really unwell, so much the better, you will not have the effort of pretending. It is only the same as sea-sickness, it will pass in a day or two.'

'A day or two!' Katharine exclaimed in dismay. 'How many days are we going to be on the road? Please, Nicholas,' she implored, and by the sound of her voice she was nearly in tears, 'it is so dark and hot in there—if I could see everything it would help—and—and enjoy myself as you are.'

'Enjoy yourself!' Nicholas was scornful. 'Do you think this is some sort of a game we are playing? Do you know what would happen if a passing troop of soldiers refused to accept our passes, or someone mistook Giles for the King? They are not unlike. We three, and Hester, are facing an ever-present danger, you are not. I am not asking you to be brave, only long-suffering.'

'I should prefer to be brave,' Katharine whispered.

'Would you? You were not very brave when you saw the soldiers at home, were you? You fainted. What sort of bravery was that? To my mind you are behaving like your father's child.'

If Nicholas had slapped his sister the effect could not have been more startling. She went scarlet and crept back to her place under the tree, where she picked silently at tiny morsels of meat and bread.

'Don't be too hard on her, she is only a child,' Giles murmured, surprised at his friend's anger.

'She is as old as Matthew,' Nicholas retorted. 'Look at what he has been through and he has never complained.'

Giles could have replied that the circumstances were quite different, but he did not want to interfere and cause more unpleasantness. Nicholas, who admired Matthew's doggedness, had never interfered in Giles's treatment of his brother, although it had been harsh enough when the boy's conceit had become unbearable.

An hour later, when the horses had been collected again, Katharine did not need to be told what to do. She ignored her brother's nod of the head and stepped into the litter without any assistance. The others mounted and began the slow journey once more.

The ride was uneventful. Their papers were accepted wherever they were shown and only at some of the inns where they stayed the nights was there any discomfort. Katharine and Hester usually shared a small room; sometimes it was clean, sometimes not, but neither grumbled, not even when their skins were swollen with the bites of fleas and lice. The other three shared the quarters of the servants and ostlers, and overheard wild rumours about the King's escape. There was a reward of a thousand pounds for information leading to his capture—fortunately, as Matthew had told Katharine, few knew what he was like—some who had assisted him had already been arrested; some rumours said he had fled to Scotland, and others, that he was disguised as a woman with a red wig and was hiding in London.

Slowly, the litter and its five travellers made their way southwards through England. When they reached Ringwood, in Hampshire, the country had become low and thickly wooded, with the great wide Avon like a ribbon across the water-meadows. They grew silent as they rode along the deserted tracks. Matthew craned his neck hoping for the first sight of the sea, but ahead was ridge upon ridge of brown heathland. To their left, like a dark cloud, stretched the Forest, patched with gold where a tree had turned yellow before its companions.

Hester quickly recognized the landmarks she had once known well. 'That is Tyrrell's Ford,' she said to Giles, pointing at the water. 'It is supposed to be where Walter Tyrrell crossed the river after the murder of King William. The farm should not be far now, just a lane leading off towards the Forest. It will be strange to see Cousin Barfutt after all these years. It will be ten years next Candlemas, when she was first widowed, and she still runs the farm even after her husband's death.'

'You have not seen her since the beginning of the war?' Giles queried, and to Hester's surprise he drew on the slack reins, pulling the horse to a halt. They were all mad, he thought, to make so many preparations, to come so many miles, and neither Nicholas nor his cousin had ever suggested that the ten years, which had been mostly taken up by civil war, might have created changes in the farm and its owner. He said so, bluntly, and that his friend's apparent eagerness to leave his home might have accounted for his lack of caution.

Hester looked worried. 'I have had a letter every Christmas and there has never been a word to show she was not loyal to the King,' she explained. 'Wait here, and we will tell Nicholas. If he agrees with your doubts we must not go on, though where we can turn to next is more than I can say.'

With Giles's assistance she slipped to the ground and went back to meet the two riders with the swaying litter.

Nicholas, who since leaving the area of his home, had regained his good humour, laughed on hearing the news.

'It is too late to go back now,' he replied. 'We shall only have to pretend a little longer until we know where Mistress Barfutt's sympathies lie. She need be told nothing for the time being. You have come to visit her and brought your sick charge for a few weeks' rest; we are your servants. Once we are on the farm we shall at least have food and shelter; we shall be near the sea and one of us can surely get in touch with someone who will help us. Kate will have the worst of it, for she will have to go on being ill and swallow all Mistress Barfutt's unpleasant remedies for making her well.'

He walked round to the side of the litter, where his sister's pale face poked between the curtains, wanting to know why they had stopped.

'Did you hear that, Kate?' he asked. 'You must not get better until we give you permission, and don't tell Mistress Barfutt who we are and why we came.' He pulled the leather across the opening again shutting out all the light and air, and remounted his horse. His expression was grave as he drew level with Giles. 'It is more than unfortunate,' he murmured to his friend, 'that the whole success of this adventure rests entirely upon the weakest among us. If Katharine fails us, we can have little hope.'

It was with curious, watchful eyes that they approached the farm and saw, beyond the thatched barns and open gateway, Mistress Sarah Barfutt urging her cows across the yard to be milked. She was a large, sturdy woman dressed in a style long out of date; the black widow's cap on her head was almost concealed by the scarf she had tied over it to protect it from the dust of the outbuildings. Hester insisted on dismounting and going to greet her cousin alone.

From where they were waiting, Giles and Nicholas tried to read what was happening. There seemed to be no great surprise on Mistress Barfutt's part at the unexpected appearance of her cousin after so many years. She kissed her boisterously on both cheeks and, still continuing to wave her stick and make strange noises in the direction of the cattle, listened to Hester's story. When all the animals were in the barn, she walked slowly with Hester back to the group by the gate. For a moment she looked the three servants up and down, in the manner, Matthew thought, that she might select a plump chicken.

'Two men and a boy, eh,' she grunted. 'I never say no to extra hands. There's still plenty to be done at this time of the year. The lad can make himself useful already and carry some of the pails to the dairy. You,' she pointed her stick at Nicholas, 'can stable your horses and house the litter. There's plenty of room at the end of the big barn. And that one,' her glance rested for longer on Giles's tall figure, 'had better bring the child indoors.'

When Giles opened the litter and bent over Katharine to pick her up, he managed a quick smile. 'Don't give in,' he whispered. 'We depend on you.'

She smiled wanly and closed her eyes as he carried her inside, following Hester and Mistress Barfutt through the kitchen and up a narrow flight of stairs between the walls at the back of the farmhouse.

They went into a small room, white-washed and clean, with two beds separated by a linen-chest. Under the tiny window was a square stool; the shelf on the wall contained a Bible, a rushlight holder and an earthenware jug.

'I've hired two of my girls out to a farmer in the Forest, so they'll not be wanting this for a while,' Mistress Barfutt explained. 'There's sheets and blankets in the chest if you'll make up the beds while I fetch up a pan of hot embers,' she said to Hester. 'She's a sickly little creature compared with the rest of you.' She nodded to Giles to place Katharine on one of the beds and then to precede her down the stairs.

Half an hour later Katharine, uncomfortablv hot in the warmed bed with the blankets piled up to her chin. was left by herself. From where she lay she could see through the little window which had been left open, although neither Sarah Barfutt nor Hester approved of fresh air in sickness; the heavy thatched eaves shut out most of the light, the panes rattled as the wind blustered against them. It seemed an everlasting wind that tore in from the sea across the inhospitable, silent wastes of marsh and heath, to be broken into gusts only when it reached the swaying forest barrier.

Chapter V

He Who Pays the Piper

KATHARINE kept still for a long time, afraid that if she moved or crept from the bed to watch from the window or listen at the door, someone would come running to ask what she was doing. She wished Hester would return and give her news of the others, especially of Mistress Barfutt's attitude, so that she would know when she would be able to give up pretending to be ill. As Nicholas had said it would, her real sickness had worn off after a few days, but, even after that, she had not enjoyed the journey. Her brother's hurtful remark had spoiled what little pleasure there might have been. Added to that, there was still the stuffiness of the litter. Nicholas, Giles, Matthew and Hester, who were out in the open air, had quickly become tanned, whereas she had grown paler, and more like the sickly child she was supposed to be. Whenever they stopped for the night at an inn, she had been carried immediately indoors, to the great curiosity of the serving-girls, and often of the inn-keeper's wife. Sometimes, the latter had not been pleased to allow illness on to her premises; sometimes, the woman had been full of sympathy and, instead of leaving Katharine and Hester alone in their room, had come up during the evening to discuss the symptoms and to suggest remedies for a cure. Then, Katharine had shed tears of frustration on Hester's sympathetic shoulder, because the evenings had been the only time when she had been able to get up and exercise her cramped limbs.

At the remembrance of the journey, Katharine stared unhappily at the little window under the eaves, where the sky was reflecting the setting sun. Gradually, as she watched, the clouds turned yellow, flame and mauve, until all the light had faded and she was in darkness. It was very quiet, and it seemed strange that, as she was supposed to be ill, she had been left alone for such a long time.

At last, there were footsteps outside, the latch rattled on the door, and Katharine turned her head expectantly, hoping that it was Hester. But Mistress Barfutt entered, shielding a candle in her hand. She closed the door, crossed the room and kindled one end of the rushlight on the shelf. Katharine's eyes followed her, and she decided, for no apparent reason, that she disliked Mistress Barfutt. Her movements were smooth, quiet with the stealth of a cat, her face, framed by the widow's cap, was expressionless, and her body was shapeless under the long, loose gown. To Katharine, she seemed solid and square, as if she had no legs, only feet fastened to the hem of her dress.

Mistress Barfutt clicked shut the window and approached the bed; her eyes, round and black, peering through the halo of light, fixed themselves on Katharine's face.

'I hoped you were asleep,' she said. 'Are you feeling better?'

Katharine nodded.

'And what made you ill in the first place? Cousin Hester has not yet had time to speak to me,' went on Mistress Barfutt, sitting on the end of the bed.

The question was unexpected, for it had not occurred to Katharine that she might be interrogated. Hester had always answered the queries of inquisitive women before, and so, falteringly, she gave Hester's answer.

'The—the soldiers at the house—they frightened me.'

'And why were they there?'

Again, Katharine hardly knew what to say. 'Why?' she whispered. 'B-because they were looking for the King, I believe.'

'Not your brother, Nicholas, by any chance?'

At the swiftness and uncanny accuracy of this question, Katharine's heart began to thump under the bedclothes. It was not right that Mistress Barfutt should be so interested in what had happened at the house, nor that she should ask Katharine about it. That part of the plan had been her brother's and Hester's responsibility — she was only supposed to lie still and look ill. She glanced at the door, hoping that it would open and Hester would come to her aid, but it remained closed.

'Why should they want to look for Nicholas?' she asked weakly.

'Because your brother was a Royalist, like all your family, though your father made a mighty poor show of his loyalty,' was the quick reply. Mistress Barfutt leaned forward and placed the candle on the chest, where its steady flame threw a light over the girl's face. 'I never knew much about your people, though I learnt plenty later,' she continued. 'When my Cousin Hester was orphaned and came to live here, she was treated like another daughter by my parents, petted and fussed because she had lost all. But was she grateful? No, she showed her gratitude by leaving as soon as she could. A letter came from your folks in the north, who hardly knew her at all, asking her to go to the great house and live as a gentlewoman — the offer was tempting and she went. No more milking in the bitter, cold mornings, no more tedious evenings spent stripping the rushes for lights — she would have servants under her to do that. Cousin Hester wanted to sew fine tapestries and read fine books, not work alongside her Cousin Sarah and end up by marrying a poor farmer.' Mistress Barfutt's jealousy burned anew at the memory. 'But when the war came, our fortunes were changed.' The faint smile of satisfaction was even more frightening to Katharine than the previous illuminating information. 'I knew which side would do the most for me, I knew which side would fight for my rights and my religion — not the King's, I can tell you. What had he ever done for me, except tax the farm to pay his debts — and what had he done for my Cousin Hester? Given her money and fine clothes, and horses to ride.'

'I am sure he has never given her anything,' Katharine murmured, searching for some words in defence of her home and her cousin.

'Stupid child, you've not the wits to understand,' Mistress Barfutt retorted. 'Now,' she said more slowly, 'you tell me why you came here.'

Katharine looked into the dark pools of her eyes, made darker by the rushlight behind. 'Because of the soldiers—they made me ill,' she said again.

'You are no more ill than I am.' Mistress Barfutt tapped the counterpane scornfully. 'You're as thin as a bean-pole, and you've a face like butter-milk, and maybe the litter has made you sick, but there's nothing the matter with you. Whatever else I may say of her, my Cousin Hester is an honest woman and she's acting a lie at the moment, and none too successfully. Why does she suddenly want to come flaunting down here in her fancy dresses, and me with one nigh twenty years old? I'll not ask her, though, and I'll not make her curious by wanting to know her business. She can go on with her mysteries, and she can think she is still calling the tune, but I will pay the piper.' She stopped abruptly and studied the pale girl in the bed. 'Are you hungry?' she asked.

'Yes,' Katharine replied, startled by the sudden change of subject.

Mistress Barfutt rose heavily, took the candle and disappeared down the stairs. Katharine blinked in the dim glow from the rushlight. She was bewildered and uneasy. If Mistress Barfutt knew she was not ill, there seemed no object in remaining in bed.

'If only Hester would come,' she murmured. 'I could tell her how jealous her cousin is, and that she wants to know why she came to the farm.' She sat up and gazed once more at the door. 'Please, Hester, come,' she whispered fervently.

Again, the footsteps on the stairs were those of Mistress

Barfutt, who was carrying, this time, a laden tray. After the days of badly-cooked food and the stuffy litter, Katharine looked eagerly at the dish of neat chicken slices folded in thick white sauce, and at the bowl of baked apples, surrounded by a sea of yellow cream, which were placed on the chest at her side.

'Before you begin,' said Mistress Barfutt, settling herself on the edge of the bed, 'you'd best tell me why my Cousin Hester came here.'

'Because I was ill,' Katharine reiterated, puzzled by the persistent return to the same question.

Mistress Barfutt shook her head. 'She had good reason for wanting you to be ill, otherwise she would have come with only one man-servant. There must be plenty of money up there, if she can bring three strapping fellows all these miles. What did she tell you when she asked you to lie in the litter?'

Katharine was silent. Even if part of their plan had been uncovered there was no need for her to betray the rest.

'Did she tell you why she wanted to come here with two grown men and a boy? Didn't it seem strange that she wanted to leave Gloucester so soon after the soldiers searching the house, and so soon after Worcester field? She wouldn't have got a pass so easily from me, if I had been one of the Justices.'

Katharine's knees hid her deepening colour.

'Maybe you're too young to know much, but I'll wager you know something. It's the papists who will help the King out of the country, and Cousin Hester is a papist. I'll mind when the baby prince was born, him who's fleeing for his life now, Queen Henrietta said he was so black she scarce liked to own him as hers. The fellow who carried you up here was swarthy enough. Have you anything to say, now?'

Katharine, startled, shook her head. 'That was Giles,' she said quickly. 'He is the boy Matthew's brother. But—

but what difference would it make to you if he were the King?'

'The difference of a thousand pounds,' came the prompt reply. 'There's a reward of a thousand pounds for anyone who can lead to the King's capture, and I would do fine with it. It would pay for a new barn, and I've been wanting a bigger dairy for months past.'

'You would sell the King, give him up for the sake of money, to buy yourself a new barn?' Katharine exclaimed incredulously, shaken out of her fear by the wickedness of the suggestion.

'Ay, he's never done anything for me.'

'He has never done anything for me,' Katharine retorted. 'The Royalists burned my home and killed my father—you have a home and everything—I have nothing, but I would never dream of harming the King—just for money—I would rather starve.'

'Maybe you'll have the opportunity,' Mistress Barfutt said sharply, angered by the girl's contempt. 'When you have answered my questions, told me why you came here, you can eat your supper, and not before.'

Katharine stared at her in horror as the woman's meaning became clear. Then she flew to her refuge of old.

'Hester will not allow you to treat me like this. When she comes up I will tell her what you have said.'

'Maybe she won't come.' Mistress Barfutt smiled grimly. 'You've not had the smallpox, have you?' she asked.

Katharine shook her head fearfully.

'If I say you have sickened for the smallpox,' Mistress Barfutt went on slowly, 'no one will come near you, and I would never let my Cousin Hester run the risk of the infection. She daren't say you are not ill, after pretending that you are, if she has anything to hide. We will see who gives in first and gives me my answer; Hester because she is worried, or you, because you are hungry.'

In the tiny, shadowed room, the stolid figure on the end of

the bed seemed all-powerful. Katharine's eyes darted to the door and to the window. How long could she go without food? How long would it be before Hester guessed that something was wrong? Did Mistress Barfutt really intend to starve her if she refused to say why they had left Gloucester? She glanced at the food, and thought of Giles, who had told her not to give in because they depended on her. She supposed that it was possible that he could be the King, after all. They might not have told her everything, because she was so timid and easily frightened. She thought of Matthew's contempt, when she had belittled the old King and his Cavaliers, though she had not meant him to take it like that, only to check his pride. Finally, she thought of Nicholas. For six years she had longed for his return, in order to try to put herself in a better position in his eyes, but something had gone wrong. Again, they had misunderstood each other because of the disparity in their ages. He had once asked why she was not older, and from that moment she had tried to appear so, failing each time her resolution had been put to the test. Now, his safety lay with her and she could not give in so easily.

'I do not want anything to eat,' she said distinctly, and, curling down on the mattress, she pulled the sheets over her head.

Mistress Barfutt grunted, rose stiffly, picked up the tray and candle and left the room. At the foot of the stairs she met Hester, who, ever since Katharine had been put to bed, had been trying to see her again. Cousin Barfutt, however, had not made that possible. She had kept Hester busy in the kitchen, helping with the preparation of the men's evening meal, and Hester had not liked to refuse her aid. She felt that, as she had arrived unexpectedly, it was only courteous to be as little trouble as possible. Whenever she had suggested that she should go up to see the sick child, Cousin Barfutt told her that she had slipped up herself, and that the child was sleeping—information which Hester had readily believed.

Mistress Barfutt held out the tray of untouched food.

'The child has eaten nothing,' she said. 'You had better not go up. It looks as though she is sickening for the smallpox.'

'The smallpox?' Hester repeated in horror. 'You should have let me go up sooner.'

Sarah Barfutt laid down the tray, took her cousin's arm and led her away from the stairs to the open window.

'That was why I would not let you,' she replied. 'I suspected something the minute I saw the child, and wanted you out of the way as quickly as possible.'

Hester, stricken by the news, but grateful for the kindness and sympathy, gazed into the dark, empty yard.

'No wonder Katharine was so sick in the litter,' she murmured, half speaking to herself. 'I did not think it should have made her so ill, but if she was sickening for this——'

Mistress Barfutt watched her curiously. She wondered if the concern were genuine or not. It gradually became plain that Hester accepted her cousin's news without question.

'I must help you to nurse her,' she suggested, when the first shock had worn off.

'That you'll not.' Mistress Barfutt was adamant. 'I've nursed it before and never taken it myself. Folks used to say that if you've had the cowpox, as I have, you'll never take the other—and there may be some truth in it for all I know. You shall have my room, and I will sleep with the child.'

Hester felt too tired to argue, although her thoughts were working quickly. If Katharine had the smallpox, it could be serious for the child, but it made no real difference to their original plan. Nicholas and Giles could go on hoping for a means of escape. As Cousin Barfutt would be occupied in nursing, there was no need to add to her worries by telling her that she had three fugitives on the farm. There had been no hint, as yet, that she was not in sympathy with the fleeing King, but, Hester felt, it was not her responsibility to ask for assistance. It was not going to be easy to speak a great deal with Nicholas, but she would have to let him know about his sister's illness as soon as possible, and ask for guidance. It was too late that evening, because the men had already finished their meal and gone to their own quarters to sleep.

It was an anxious night for Hester, trying to rest in her cousin's large four-poster bed with the thick, dark hangings drawn around to keep out all the draughts. She was worried about Katharine, for the child had never before been separated from her, and was sure to be frightened and bewildered in her illness in the strange surroundings.

The following morning, she waited for Mistress Barfutt to return from the tiny room, which, because it had been intended for the use of servants, could only be reached by the stairs between the walls from the kitchen. She watched in concern, as her cousin, grim-faced, placed untouched bowls of food upon the table.

'How is she?' Hester asked timidly.

'There is no mistaking the spots, now,' Cousin Barfutt replied. 'I will burn her clothes so that the infection won't spread, and take these to board up the window—the daylight will be bad for her eyes.' As she spoke, she picked up some slats of wood which she had brought earlier from the dairy.

'I ought to speak to my own servants and warn them of the danger,' Hester suggested, hastily.

'They are in the fields, and you will have to wait until this evening,' was the gruff answer.

Hester affectionately took her cousin's hand, and thought that it was modesty on the older woman's part which caused her to look in the opposite direction and not meet her own warm gaze.

'You are doing so much,' she said gratefully. 'I know the

child could not have a better nurse. I can only pray that she will be all right. She is not strong.'

Mistress Barfutt hastily withdrew her fingers, and whisked hammer and nails from a drawer in the dresser.

'She is a deal stronger than I took her for,' she muttered, as she returned resolutely up the narrow staircase.

Chapter VI

An Unexpected Journey

KATHARINE lay curled in a ball, huddled under the bedclothes. She had lost count of the time because the window had been sealed so that the room was in complete darkness. She only knew that she was terribly hungry, and that it was more than hunger, now, a great void, a dull ache in her head, and when she left the bed the darkness swam about her.

'I cannot hold out any longer,' she said to herself. 'When she brings another meal I shall have to give in.'

She had just refused a tempting broth with dainty squares of crisped bread around the bowl. At its side had been a little dish of syllabub made from milk and honey, which she felt she could have eaten — anything more solid would have made her ill. Katharine wriggled miserably at the thought, and at the remembrance of Mistress Barfutt, candle in hand, leaning over her bed smiling gently, and in the kindest tones trying to persuade her to taste.

'Why does not anyone guess that something is wrong?' Katharine asked aloud.

It seemed impossible to think that Hester really believed Mistress Barfutt's story and would not, somehow, come to her help. She gnawed her fingers and tried to make her wandering brain concentrate on a way out other than giving in to Mistress Barfutt and so betraying all of them. It was Giles now, that she was most concerned about. Nicholas, if he lived after her betrayal, might one day forgive her, although he had never forgiven his father. But Giles might be the King, and what would all the Royalists say, what would the whole world say, if she betrayed her King? Like father, like child. She shuddered at the memory and sat up. There must be something she could do. If she screamed for help everyone would think she was delirious; there was no paper, no pen; she could not open the window and attract someone's attention, but, on the other hand, she knew the door was not locked.

There was no way to the room except by going through the kitchen; there was a half-door which was usually kept fastened across the foot of the stairs. The door of Katharine's room was on the latch, for Mistress Barfutt, knowing no one would go near the child because of the infection and having removed all Katharine's clothes, felt that there was no risk of her scheme being discovered. With heavy trays to carry up and down it was easier to leave the door so that she could push it with her foot.

Katharine slid from the bed and groped unsteadily across the bare boards to feel for the latch. The door creaked and opened a few inches, and, as she stood there, her heart pounding, wild ideas flitted through her mind. She had no shoes, no clothes, only the shift she was wearing. The passage led to the stairs which went straight into the kitchen where the farm-hands, milkmaids, Mistress Barfutt and Hester might be at any hour of the day. She could not, as she was, go in broad daylight, risking whoever might be there, in order to find Giles or Nicholas. Even if Hester saw her she might think she was running about mad in her illness. She could not go at night, for Mistress Barfutt shared her room, sleeping lightly and little in the bed at her side.

To have no privacy had at first been worse than being hungry. A room shared with Hester, who had been her companion for so long, was very different from a room shared with Sarah Barfutt. Katharine had watched at night, out of curiosity, ill-mannered though she knew it was, as layer after layer of gown and petticoat had been discarded until the great boned corsets were unlaced, and with a sigh of pleasure the large woman had allowed her ample body to roll naked into the creaking bed. Katharine had turned her back on such immodesty for Hester always wore a nightshift, and a cap to cover her hair.

The passage and stairs were quiet and Katharine closed the door gently and went back to bed. If she was to find anyone to help her she would have to go out as she was. 'When will the kitchen be empty and the cobbled yard deserted?' she asked herself. It had been bustling with activity when they had arrived but, she remembered with eagerness, there had been a long, almost unbelievable silence after she had been put to bed and Mistress Barfutt had left with the warming pan, saying she had to go to the dairy. Katharine lay under the blankets flushed with the excitement of a possible plan.

'I shall hear the cows come in for milking although I cannot tell the time,' she thought. 'I can listen until I think Mistress Barfutt has gone to the dairy. While the cows are in the sheds being milked, there will not be anyone about, the men ought still to be in the fields. If I can hide where I might see Nicholas as he comes in, I can tell him what is happening. Perhaps he will know what I can say so that I can have something to eat,' she added wistfully.

The hours dragged, Katharine's ears grew tired straining for the tinkling bells as the cattle were driven in from the fields. When she heard them she slipped from the bed and crouched at the shuttered window, listening to the cries of the milkmaids, and when they were silent she waited at the half-open door, ready to dart back to bed if Mistress Barfutt's step approached the bottom stair.

All was quiet, and so, bare-footed, clutching her loose shift to her waist, she tiptoed into the passage. The strips of worn flag she could see across the kitchen floor below looked strangely light after her dark room. She had expected that it would be later in the day, but the sun was striking through the low windows on to the bright pans in the hearth. A shadow fell across the pans and Katharine flattened herself against the walls of the stairs, praying it would come no nearer.

Mistress Barfutt moved into the opening. She was humming tunelessly, twisting her skirt to her waist until a length of thick wrinkled hose showed above her wooden pattens. She lifted a three-legged skillet from the fire and then selected several copper skimmers from the rack above. Still humming, she clattered slowly to the outer door and Katharine, stepping down cautiously, watched her disappear past the window towards the dairy.

Katharine slipped the bolt on the half-door and crept into the kitchen. It was cool and neat, the tables scrubbed white, the long benches pushed to the sides and all Mistress Barfutt's bread shovels, pans and cauldrons glistening in their rightful places. Through the doorway she could see the empty yard, cobbled and muddy. A huge heap of straw and muck swept from the steadings was steaming in the middle with the hens scratching hopefully around. To the left, was the gate leading from the farm, and beyond it, a group of barns, some closed and one with its great doors swinging wide showing the carts inside. If she could hide there, Katharine thought, it was well away from the house and in the opposite direction to the dairy. She paused on the threshold for a final reassurance that no one was about, pressing her cold toes over the rounded stones of the step before sidling along the skirting of grass which bordered the track to the gate. She hovered at the gate, her frightened eyes darting at the buildings, the rough ground, the yard behind and the deeply rutted lane. Then she ran for the shelter of the open barn.

It was then that Matthew saw her. Coming round the corner of the yard, bearing a yoke on his shoulders from which dangled two full buckets of water, he caught a glimpse of a white figure which darted from the sunlit path into the gloom of the barn. He hurried forward, heedless, in his excitement, of the water splashing down his legs.

'That is Katharine,' he whispered incredulously. He set down the pails and stealthily followed to hide behind a stack of logs to watch. She was supposed to be ill, he thought, his anger rising, and as Nicholas had said, holding their lives in the palms of her hands, and there she was playing truant from her bed while everyone else was working. If she was unable to put up with two days of discomfort what hope was there for them to find a way of escape? Giles had told him how patient they must be because he had been tempted to grumble at the inaction. It might be some time before they could find a boatman loyal enough and willing to run the risks involved.

Matthew shifted his position and stared across into the shadowy barn where the white figure, like an aimless moth, flitted uncertainly among the carts. Should he speak to her and tell her in what danger she was putting them all? Matthew shrugged his shoulders. She would probably scream or faint and bring everyone's attention to the pair of them. In any case, Nicholas had warned her before and asked for her co-operation; if she chose to ignore her brother's wishes she could take the consequences of her foolishness and be punished for it. He would not leap to her defence and Giles might realize that the colourless little creature was more selfish than he supposed. Matthew was determined that none of them should suffer, and at the earliest opportunity he would let Nicholas know what he had seen.

'Boy! Where's that boy?' It was Mistress Barfutt's voice from the yard and at the sound Matthew sprang back to his pails. He, too, disliked Mistress Barfutt, for she had kept him continually at work from the time he got up until he went to bed at night. 'They are waiting in the dairy for that water,' she shouted, as Matthew staggered towards her.

The sound had frightened Katharine, for out of the corner of his eye Matthew had seen the white shape fluttering up one of the carts and disappearing between the sacks piled there.

Katharine, sweat pouring from her forehead with fear, burrowed among the sacks, praying that Mistress Barfutt would not see her. The approach of the wooden pattens was terrifying. They echoed on the stones and thudded on the grass like a great shire horse, until Katharine realized to her horror that it was a horse, and a man, accompanying Mistress Barfutt into the barn. The cart rocked as the shafts were raised and the horse was backed between them.

'You'll be home before nightfall if you don't dawdle,' said Mistress Barfutt, her head barely a foot below where Katharine was hiding.

The man grunted, obviously not pleased at being sent out at such an hour. 'Come up, there,' he roared, catching at the animal's bridle.

The cart shuddered and with a sudden jerk rolled out of the barn. Katharine clung to the sacks, not knowing whether to stay or cry out that she was there, but the cart gathered speed and lurched out into the open country.

It was a short-lived burst of energy. Once beyond Mistress Barfutt's hearing, the horse slackened to a comfortable walk with the carter singing a low, mournful chant to the rhythm of his animal's hoofs.

Unable to tell where she was going, Katharine knew by the bumps and rattles of the wheels that they were passing over stony ground on what seemed to be a road with few curves or slopes. At first she kept still, too numbed by what had happened to do more than grip the sack nearest to her for support and comfort. Gradually, as the immediate fear wore off, she began to think of the end of the journey; she had no idea where the carter was going, possibly a mill because there was a mealy, floury smell about the contents of the cart, and if he went to a mill the cart would have to be unloaded and she would be discovered. Somehow, she thought, she would have to slip down unnoticed, either before their destination or when the wagon halted. As it was barely dusk she was too frightened of being seen to risk jumping on to the open road. That would mean she would have to return to the farm along the track, if she could find the way, go through the yard to the kitchen which would soon be filled with labourers, and up the stairs to her room. An undertaking which would be impossible, especially if, by then, Mistress Barfutt had carried up her supper and discovered she had disappeared. The second plan seemed the safest. As soon as the cart stopped, and before the carter had time to reach the ground, she would have to drop down, hide near by while he unloaded, and clamber up again when he was ready to drive off. In that way, she thought nervously, she might return to find Giles or Nicholas, for the warning to them was all that really mattered. What would be the result of her action from Mistress Barfutt's point of view, she dared not think.

The carter did not appear to have listened to his instructions about 'dawdling' and being 'home by nightfall', because he was making no attempt to hurry and the daylight was fading quickly, Katharine, realizing that the darkness would be her greatest help, tried not to worry any longer about her absence from the little shuttered room. She squeezed an arm between the sacks and made a gap through which she could watch the road. She saw the thatched roofs of cottages, an old stone cross and later the edge of a long bridge over a wide stretch of water. There was a sharp turn into a dim, leafy lane, and after a crack of the whip the cart went rocking violently downhill.

With a shout from its driver it swayed to an abrupt halt, sending the bulging sacks heavily against Katharine, who tried frantically to push her way nearer to the side. There was a jerk, a clatter of boots on cobbles as the carter dropped to the ground, and a moment later a yellow beam of light slid from a slowly opened doorway to rest on the waiting group.

'I told the old woman you wouldn't be pleased to see me at this hour,' grumbled the carter to the unseen person who had come out in answer to his call. 'She won't use the miller at Sopley, says he's a rogue and overcharged her last year. Do you want any help?' The offer was not convincing.

'It's late now. I'll stack them for the night,' was the reply. 'There's ale inside. Help yourself.'

The carter grunted his thanks and for a second his shadow blocked the shaft of light. Katharine held her breath, watching through the gap as the man paused at the foot of a small flight of steps. Her plan seemed to be going better than she had hoped, for when they were both indoors, drinking each other's health, she would seize her opportunity, slip down and hide until he was ready to return home. The man disappeared through the bright entrance, pulling the door behind him. Katharine blinked in the sudden darkness and moved quickly; the horse shifted uneasily, making the cart quiver, the whole framework shook as some heavy object was flung on to it, a sack was tossed aside, there was a muffled exclamation, and Katharine crouched terrified, as a man's figure towered above her.

Chapter VII

The Miller of Place

KATHARINE did not move, nor, for some minutes, did the man. Then, 'You had better get down,' he said.

She obeyed, but he gave her no help. He waited at the side of the cart until she had reached the ground.

'Over there,' he said and turned his head in the direction of a doorway under a low roof, to the right of where the carter had disappeared.

The stones were cold to Katharine's bare feet and the fresh night wind stirred the thin folds of her shift as she ran for the shelter. The room behind was full of mysterious shapes, there was the smell of dust and meal, there was the faint drip of water, the unmistakable sound of a flowing river, and she had not the courage to enter. She stood on the threshold with her arms clasped round her shivering body watching the man who, with the rhythm of one used to the work, was quickly removing the sacks from the cart to the cobbled square on which she waited.

The carter appeared in the lighted doorway and came slowly down the steps. 'That was good ale, Master Miller,' he said, and in gratitude heaved down the final sack. He climbed on to the cart. 'Come up, there,' he roared, his voice echoing against the mill wall. The horse turned and, instinctively knowing that its day's work was done, that home lay at the end of the road and that it was drawing an empty wagon, set off at a lively pace.

Katharine, seeing her one hope of return melting into the dark lane, scrambled hysterically into the open.

'I want to go back,' she cried, bursting into tears. 'I must go back, I must.'

'You should have thought of that before you came,' the miller replied, as he tossed the last sack into place.

'I didn't want to come—I had to hide somewhere or she would have seen me. Please let me go back——'

'You go indoors and calm yourself down,' he said brusquely. The tears pouring down her cheeks, Katharine fled to the steps and hesitated in the doorway. The miller, following, gave her a slight push into the room and fastened the door behind her. He went straight to the hearth and began banking the fire up with turfs.

'What are you doing in your shift?' he asked, again abruptly.

For a moment, Katharine had forgotten how little she was wearing. Her cold, damp fingers spread over the dainty material of her nightgown as she looked down at herself, standing in the full light of the candles from the table. She backed to the door, her eyes searching the shadows to see how many others there might be peering at her. The room was quiet and still, and empty except for the miller who was bending over the hearth, and his head was turned to his task. Although he had asked the question, he was not impatient over the length of the pause before she replied.

'I—I ran away,' she whispered. There was no other reason she could give. 'I—ran away—because I was supposed to be ill—and I am not.' The memory of the past situation, the disappearing cart and her discovery by the miller, once more obliterated all thoughts of her clothing, and the words tumbled out between renewed sobs. 'She—Mistress Barfutt—wouldn't give me anything to eat unless I told her why we came to the farm—and Giles and Nicholas said I was to pretend to be ill—and then—then, she said I had the smallpox and—please let me go back,' she implored. 'I must tell them what she is going to do—and—and if they find I have gone, they will think I couldn't pretend any longer. Nicholas says I am a coward like my father—and he was shot because he wasn't brave enough to hold the house, and I don't want to be like him — I don't want to be like him.' She ended in a wail of misery, overcome by the thought of her brother and the dreadful conclusions he would reach on finding she had left the farm.

'You will be warmer if you come nearer the fire,' was all the miller said, as if he had not heard anything of her story.

He gave her a piece of coarse cloth with which Katharine gratefully rubbed her streaming nose and eyes. Then she took a nervous step towards the hearth.

'If you are afraid of the cats, I will move them,' he added, seeing her hesitation.

For the first time, Katharine noticed the tumbled mixture of fur, which lay in front of the fire, like a thick, gently moving rug — ginger, tabby and white. Three pairs of eyes, golden, yellow and pale green, opened to watch her bare toes creeping past them to the edge of the stones.

She knelt on the ground, her shoulder resting against the wooden beams surrounding the chimney and her face turned to the miller. He was watching her, now, too, with a strange calm curiosity and interest. He was tall, as straight and slim as a spear, his hair white or fair in the candlelight, powdered with dust from the mill, his clothes equally misty, breeches, shirt, stockings and shoes softly clouded in a fine yellow film, which made him seem almost a creature of her imagination.

'When did you last eat?' he asked, showing that he had understood something of her incoherent sentences.

'I don't remember,' she whispered. 'It might have been yesterday — it was a long time ago.'

He poured milk from a jug into a pan which he put on the fire. When it was warmed he tipped in a spoonful of honey and pieces of bread. He placed the pan on the floor at her side and waited in silence until she had eaten as much as she could.

'Who are you?' he asked.

His questions were so simple and direct that it did not occur to Katharine to lie to him.

'Katharine Lambert,' she replied softly.

There was a pause before he made the next query. 'And you have a brother Nicholas up at Virgin Farm?'

Katharine hesitated. Had she told him that Nicholas was her brother? If she had, it was something no one else knew, for if Mistress Barfutt discovered that, the betrayal was complete. She stared down at the empty pan in her hand; the food

had temporarily eased her aching head and now she wondered what she had said in that burst of panic when the carter had driven away. She knew her silence was as much a confirmation of the question as if she had replied 'Yes'.

She looked again at the miller, who was beyond the range of the candlelight, in the shadows which hugged the wall. He appeared to be a part of his furniture, the dresser with its rows of pewter and wooden platters, the shelf containing the books, the table with its half-finished meal. She looked back at the warm mat of fur at her feet, where an occasional pink tongue flickered and the contented purr throbbed with the river outside. The room was full of drowsiness and peace. Against her will, Katharine let her head droop and her eyes close.

In the distance a horse was being ridden slowly, the regular hoof beats, like the ticking of a clock, rocked in her sleep. They grew louder and louder, thudding in her ears until with a crash she was shaken into wakefulness. Someone hammered at the door, the pan clattered from her grasp and Katharine sprang terrified to her feet.

'Stay where you are,' said the miller sharply, and went to open the door.

'Any chance of a lodging for the night?' asked a jovial voice, and into the room stepped a stocky, ruddy, good-looking man. He was of middle age, dressed simply in a buff-coloured suit, riding boots and tall hat.

Katharine wrapped herself in her arms trying to hide her scanty clothing.

'What a mockery of a town!' the stranger exclaimed. 'One street, one inn, and that too full of fleas to allow room for travellers, one castle nearly in ruins, one priory well-nigh deserted, one long, treacherous bridge and two rivers too deep to ford.'

'You have come from the west across Iford bridge, then?' asked the miller.

'Yes, and I want lodgings for a week or more. I'm a merchant interested in the possibilities of this harbour for trading. If you can give me a room and meals, I will be little trouble to you in your work, Master Miller. I can pay well, if that is of any consideration.' The man stood, hands on hips, hat on the back of his head, smiling across the room. Then he noticed Katharine shrinking in the corner of the hearth, trying to hide behind the miller. 'Why,' he went on, 'I did not see there was anyone else here. Pack the child off to bed and we can talk business. There is stabling for my horse too, if you are agreeable.'

The miller glanced at Katharine. 'You had better go up to bed again, Kate,' he said deliberately.

Katharine stared, eyes wide, cheeks pale.

The miller shrugged his shoulders apologetically. 'She is afraid of the mice,' he explained. 'They come in from the mill in spite of the cats. She is a little town-bred mouse herself, my sister's child, and not used to the ways of the country. I will go up with her. Make yourself comfortable—there's ale, plenty of bread and cheese if you are hungry. Come here, Katharine.' He took her limp fingers firmly in his and led her through another door, which he closed after them.

Katharine tried to wriggle from his grip. 'Why didn't you tell him?' she gasped. 'I am not staying here—I want to go back—they may be killed and it will all be my fault——'

'Be quiet,' he hissed. 'You are coming upstairs and if you struggle I shall have to carry you.'

After that threat, Katharine allowed herself to be guided up two flights of stairs, in complete darkness, to a tiny room at the top of the mill.

'There is a bed when you want to lie down,' he told her. 'Don't try jumping out of the window, you would fall into the river. I shall lock the door or you will come wandering down to us again. Don't cry out, our guest will only think you are afraid of the mice. There are no mice really,' he added, a glimmer of humour in his voice. 'The cats are better hunters than I would admit. I will come back later to bring you a blanket.'

Then he left her and Katharine heard his footsteps growing fainter and fainter. She stood in the middle of the room, afraid to move and too tired even to cry, except to give one last shivering sob. The man was neither rough nor unkind, but the implication to the stranger that she was his niece was frightening. She longed for someone to protect and pet her as they had always done in the past—Nicholas or Hester should have come to her help—and most of all she wanted the re-assuring presence of her old battered, wooden doll.

At the thought of the doll Katharine blushed, a blush which sent a warm glow over her whole body, for if Nicholas knew what she was thinking he would feel more than shame for her. A grown girl of thirteen crying for a wooden doll! She could imagine the look on his face, and Matthew's turned-up nose tilting the higher in his scorn, and Giles's mild look of surprise and reproach because he had thought better of her.

It seemed so much easier to be brave whenever she remembered Giles. King or not, he always expected the best of her and it would be humiliating to let him down. She sniffed. Perhaps the miller had been wise in his behaviour. If he had told the truth it would have needed a long explanation which she would not have wanted to give. Would he let her go back to the farm in the morning? It would be almost too late, for, by then, Mistress Barfutt would have discovered her absence.

'If Mistress Barfutt has given out to everyone that I have the smallpox,' Katharine murmured aloud, 'she cannot tell them that I have disappeared, because they will know that I would have been too ill to move. In that case,' she added, a smile curving her lips, 'she will have to go on pretending that I am upstairs in bed.'

It was comforting to think that Mistress Barfutt would be in difficulties herself, but not so comforting to think that her own sudden flight might lead the widow to believe that her suspicions about the reason for the journey were correct. Katharine moved to the bed and crouched on the hard straw mattress trying to keep warm and listening to the soft wash of the river below.

She must have fallen asleep, for she was awakened suddenly by a light shining on her face. It was the miller, standing at the door, with a lantern in his hand and a blanket over his arm.

'Wrap yourself in this,' he said. 'I want to talk to you.'

He sat down on the other end of the bed and placed the

lantern between them, waiting, elbows on knees, looking at the ground while Katharine swathed herself in the warm woollen cloth. As he was silent for some time, almost as though he had forgotten she was there, she was able to study him more closely. He was older than she had first thought, the nearness of the candle showing up the fine lines around his eyes. Unexpectedly, he turned his head and caught her looking at him. He smiled at her embarrassment.

'You cannot go back to the farm, Katharine, until you have some clothes,' he began quietly. 'Those you shall have tomorrow from Mistress Tuck, the woman who comes in every day to cook for me. Whether, when you have them, you will still want to return, rests with you. You must be able to see for yourself that it will not be easy. You and I, Kate,' he spoke gravely, 'have got to trust one another, because we both have something to hide. You said a number of unwise things this evening when you were frightened, which I could easily piece together. I want to know more about you and your brother at the farm.'

'I cannot tell you, I am afraid to,' Katharine murmured, thinking of Nicholas's warning. 'It will only make everything worse. I say things when I am frightened that I do not really mean—and do things I don't want to.'

He smiled at the evasion of his question. 'You have spent most of your life being afraid of something, haven't you? If you have a fear you must either conquer it or learn to live with it; you cannot go through the rest of your days blaming all your actions on to one incident which happened when you were small. You cannot blame all your fears and misdeeds on to your father. That is the coward's way out,' he continued, 'to shirk the responsibility of your own behaviour and pretend you do not know right from wrong. You are old enough now to stop living in the shadow of your father's disgrace and to have the strength of will to form your own character.'

Katharine's cheeks burned uncomfortably. Had she told him that her father and the soldiers were the cause of her babyish conduct? The miller's blunt attack made her more ashamed of herself than Hester's attitude that she was still in the nursery, Matthew's contempt or Giles's sympathy.

'I do not expect you to speak first,' he said, seeing that she was unable to reply. 'So that you may trust me I shall have to put my life into your hands, believing that you will not betray my confidence.' As she did not answer he seemed to accept her co-operation, and went on speaking in the low tones he had used ever since coming into the room. He leaned against the wall at the back of the bed and folded his arms. 'Earlier in the war there was fighting here in Christchurch in which I was involved. I was wounded and left for dead in the grounds of the Priory. There, the miller of Place, this mill, found me and carried me home to his wife here. They hid me and nursed me until eventually I was able to return to the Royalist forces.' He paused as if to allow Katharine to understand the significance of that sentence. 'When our former King, Charles I, was martyred, it seemed that the country had gone too far in its rebellion and the only hope of salvation for his son's supporters was to flee abroad and bring about his restoration from there. As a fugitive, I came here again two years ago, hoping that Master Tuck, the miller, and his wife would hide me until a boat could take me to France. The old miller was dying—I used to sit with him during the day while his wife and a hired man did the work of the mill. He told me it was not right for all those loyal to the King to run from the country like rats from a sinking ship. "If England is not to sink," he said, "someone must stay behind to mend the leak." You follow what I am saying?' he asked Katharine.

She nodded. No longer afraid, no longer feeling the strangeness of her situation, she was more than contented that she should be spoken to as an adult. No one had ever done that before.

'Old Master Tuck,' the miller continued, 'wanted to know how all the fleeing Royalists were going to occupy themselves abroad. The mill meant more to him than just a way of earning his daily wage. It was part of his life and faith, it ground the flour for bread, and people needed his earthly bread as much as the spiritual. To him, it was part of God's plan and therefore part of eternity. The water that turned the wheel never ceased, it went on, before him and after him, and he was only a tiny cog in God's purpose. He knew that if even one cog in his great wheel were missing all the machinery would stop. In the same way it was his duty to see that his life served its purpose and he did not leave it empty by running away. "Someone must stay in the country and work," he told me. "So many of you Cavaliers want only pleasure and amusement. Get down to the earth and find satisfaction there. That is why Master Cromwell has beaten you. He was a farmer, most of his soldiers are farmers, yeomen, shoemakers, and not too proud to use their hands and minds in simple occupations."' The miller paused again, and the sound of the river flowed into the little room. 'He died—and I stayed, a poor replacement for it takes a lifetime to make a good miller; but he gave me something I had never discovered in the pleasures of the Court or the excitement of the war—faith, an ability to live alone and not to be afraid of my own company.' He bent forward so that his face was once more in the light of the lantern. 'Will you trust me now, Katharine?' he asked. 'If I can help you, I will.'

For a moment Katharine did not speak. As in the room below she felt the whole situation was unreal. It was impossible that she, always so timid, always protected by Hester, should be curled on a bed, wrapped in a blanket, listening to the strange story of the unknown miller of Place. It was odd, that he, like Giles, should be able to give her confidence. He had quelled her tears by ignoring them; in a few blunt sentences he had made her ashamed of fears which she had always been encouraged to blame on to the day her father had died, and he had told her she was old enough to be responsible for her own behaviour. Added to that, he had revealed who he was —a Royalist, who because of an old man's scorn had been willing to give up his hope of a cultured life abroad and stay in England to try to restore sanity to his country.

He was waiting for her reply, unhurried and patient. Katharine smiled, as she had smiled at Matthew the first morning on the stairs when he had rebuffed her friendship. Then, gravely, she began to tell him why she was at Virgin Farm with Nicholas, Giles and Matthew, when her real home was in Gloucestershire.

Chapter VIII

Mistress Barfutt Writes a Letter

THE same evening on his return to the loft above the barn where he slept with Giles and Nicholas, Matthew was confronted by his solemn-faced brother. Nicholas, lying propped on his elbow on one of the straw mattresses, also looked pale and serious.

'Mistress Hester has just been able to give us news of Katharine,' Giles explained. 'Evidently the child was really not well during the journey in the litter and she has developed the smallpox.' He waited for the boy's reaction to the dreadful news.

'I don't believe you,' Matthew exploded.

'Why not?' Giles asked grimly, thinking of Nicholas who already regretted his sharp-tongued treatment of his sister.

'Because I saw her myself this afternoon, flitting across the yard into the big barn.' He went on to tell them what he had seen.

'Why didn't you speak to her?' Giles asked in exasperation.

Matthew's feet fidgetted uncomfortably.

'I can tell you why,' his brother continued, his low voice vibrating over the emptiness of the loft. 'You hoped she would get into trouble, didn't you? From the very first you had no liking for her because she was small and weak, not used to the ways of boys, and it gave you a sense of power to treat her with contempt.' He caught hold of Matthew by his jacket and swung him into the middle of the floor. 'What have we here,' he said to Nicholas, 'but a child?' The tone was withering. 'A child, who is entirely occupied with his own petty pleasures and jealousies, too young, apparently, to realize that his brother may hang for his folly. Would you care to see me and Nicholas drawn and quartered while still alive because you wanted to pick a quarrel with a girl?'

Matthew cowed before the biting sarcasm. He had never seen his brother so angry. 'I didn't think it would affect your lives,' he muttered.

'Obviously not, but it is not my life that I am so concerned with, it is the state of your conscience. What have I been living with these past months? What have your upbringing and education taught you? Nothing but selfishness, to gratify yourself at the expense of a helpless girl.' Here Nicholas felt shamed. 'To have no sense of loyalty, to do what you wish, when you wish regardless of the consequences. When you say your prayers to-night,' Giles's voice was barely above a whisper but every word was clear, 'instead of gabbling the meaningless ritual which is usual, you should repeat some part of the Litany and apply it to yourself—"from all blindness of heart, from pride, vainglory and hypocrisy, from envy, hatred and malice, and all uncharitableness, Good Lord, deliver me."'

He released his grip and Matthew turned away quickly, to roll, face to the wall, on his own pallet. He rankled with fury because Nicholas had witnessed his disgrace.

Nicholas ignored the scene. He was contemplating the criss-cross shadows cast by their lantern on the rafters of the barn.

'Someone must be telling lies,' he said thoughtfully. 'Why should Dame Barfutt say Kate has the smallpox when she is well enough to be running about the yard?'

That was a problem Mistress Barfutt spent a sleepless night trying to solve, pacing the little shuttered room, her mind searching without result to know how the child had disappeared so completely.

'I'd not meant to starve her,' she mused, pulling again at

the covers of the deserted bed. 'She must have known I wouldn't have starved her. I only meant to frighten her into telling me why they came—perhaps she didn't know—perhaps they came because she wasn't well after all. No, I'll not believe that, there's something behind it which they didn't tell her and she's got scared because she's nothing to say to me and thinks I'll starve her to death. But where's she gone? If anyone sees her and she tells what I said, that is the end of my chance of the thousand pounds—for it is something to do with the King, I'll be bound.'

She arose early in the morning and made a thorough inspection of the yard and barns before returning to the dairy. There, she started pounding the butter, which was a rhythmical process and needed little effort of concentration, as she knew from the swishing of the milk left in the churn when her work was finished. The milkmaids coming in later, saw that their stern mistress was unusually pre-occupied and their chatter and giggles became more noisy.

Mistress Barfutt went over again all her actions of the previous evening, paying particular attention to the length of time the kitchen had remained empty. 'If she slipped down because she was hungry and ran up again, I could have understood it, though I never thought she would have the courage to leave the room. But there's no food missing, not even a bunch of herbs from a hook. She didn't go through the still-room because young Alice was there all the time labelling the crocks, and the girl said she saw no one all the afternoon, although I had to be careful what I asked her. She's not hiding in the yard because I searched every shed, sty, loft and barn myself, which put the fear of the Lord into the hands because they thought they must have been shirking their work.' She chuckled at the memory. 'And she'll never have gone far in daylight in just her nightgown.' The butter flopped thickly in the churn and Mistress Barfutt's strong, brown arms went regularly up and down. 'When she left the room, the men would have been coming in from the fields and they would have seen her, and no one left the farm between milking and nightfall—aha—yes, they did.' The butter missed a turn and the work went on more slowly. 'Barney went to the mill with a wagon-load of grain. If she was in among the sacks he would have seen her.'

The butter-making was abruptly left to a girl while Mistress Barfutt found Barney in the stables and questioned him. He had to admit that on arrival at the mill he had gone indoors to drink the miller's health, leaving the miller to unload the cart. He had then driven straight home.

Mistress Barfutt was not defeated by this information. She returned to the farmhouse, to her own small, dark parlour and sat at the table, which held all her lists and accounts, and tried to compose a letter to the miller of Place. It had to be carefully worded. She told him that she was looking after a child from Sopley, whose mother was ill and whose father was a pedlar. The previous evening the child had disappeared from the farm, and she very much feared that she might have run away to find her father, who travelled in the villages towards Poole. It sounded convincing when Mistress Barfutt read it through and she ended by asking the miller if he had seen the girl while unloading the cart. She was hopeful of a satisfactory reply. She knew nothing of the miller at Christchurch. He had taken over from old Miller Tuck, but was certainly not so reliable in his work; he could not dress his own stones as most did, he was erratic, but he was honest, which was more than the millers of Throop or Knapp.

Having sealed the letter, she called Matthew from the yard and told him to borrow a pony from Barney, take the letter to the mill below the Priory at Christchurch and bring back a reply. Matthew obeyed that order with more speed than he had done any of the others. It was the first opportunity that had occurred for one of them to go near the sea, and he desperately hoped that, after his earlier disgrace, he might be able to learn something of the shipping in the harbour.

He went off revelling in his unexpected freedom, following the track which ran near the slow-moving Avon. The ground was flat, only on his right a low hill rising from the meadows and heath behind Christchurch; to his left, as before, was the dark line of the Forest. Matthew whistled, flicking with his newly-cut switch the flies from his pony's ears and the gossamer from the hedges. When he reached the bridge at Christchurch he rode down the path by the mill stream, passing the Priory in its wooded grounds, and on, seemingly out into the isolation of the marshes and the lonely stretch of water where the Avon met the Stour.

As he drew near the mill he could hear the rumbling of the machinery and smell the dust in the air. The great wheel, draped with bright weed which glistened in the sunlight, was turning slowly, the water showering from its dark framework like pieces of a sparkling rainbow. Two little windows like hollow eyes stared above, and two more at a higher level gazed into the blue sky. Matthew dismounted and fastened his pony to a stake in the ground. He crossed the yard, which was paved with a mixture of cobbles and old grind-stones, to the low porch over an open door. The porch was filled with sacks, on one of which sat a tabby cat washing its paws. Matthew looked through the door into the square room beyond, which was throbbing with the vibration of the various wheels. The stream turned the wheel outside and that turned the heavy pit-wheel, which caught in its wooden cogs smaller wheels and the shaft which made the grind-stone revolve on the floor above. There were sacks spaced neatly under a long beam, and into one of these sacks, through a narrow chute, poured a steady flow of ground grain. The miller was standing at the side letting the flour trickle between his fingers to test how the stones had been running.

'Good day, sir,' Matthew called, shouting above the noise. 'I have a letter from Mistress Barfutt of Virgin Farm.'

The miller straightened his back, brushed his hands down

his already powdered breeches and came towards him. He nodded a greeting, took the letter and broke the seal. As he read he began to smile and Matthew could not help wondering what the grim Mistress Barfutt had written that could be so amusing.

'No,' said the miller when he had finished. 'Tell her I took nothing from the cart but sacks.' He seemed to hesitate, looking at Matthew as if he wanted to say more, but he changed his mind, stuffed the letter in his pocket and went back to his work.

Matthew, thankful that his task had been carried out so quickly, was determined to make the most of his time and explore the harbour. He remounted the pony, rode back to the bridge and took the Lymington track, which skirted the marsh. Soon, spread before him, he saw the wide expanse of shimmering blue water surrounded by the shimmering, swaying green of the grasses and tall rushes bent in the wind. Behind, small and fairy-like, rose the honey-coloured tower of the Priory.

Near the water's edge, his boots squelching in the soft ground, a man was standing with his horse. Matthew approached cautiously.

'Is that the sea?' he asked.

The man turned and smiled. 'Almost,' he agreed. 'It is the harbour. The sea is outside that narrow gap.'

Matthew's eyes followed the pointing finger along the curve of a hill in the distance, which hugged the harbour like an arm, and saw the few yards of water before another arm, topped with pines, hugged the other side.

'I thought there would be more ships,' he said, noticing the few barges and flat boats anchored in the shelter.

'There should be—it's a fine basin with two rivers pouring into it, but it is hardly used at all.' The tone was slightly aggrieved. 'I think they fish from the little hamlet at the harbour mouth, but the tides and waters are wasted. I suppose the town must have a trade of some kind and there must be coasting vessels sailing to near-by ports. Are you interested in the sea?' the stranger asked abruptly.

'In ships, yes,' Matthew replied and, trying not to appear over eager, added, 'although I know little about them.'

The man tapped his whip against his boot. 'I have come here to study this harbour,' he said. 'It should be able to take larger vessels than this. I want to know about the tides, depth of water and position of sandbanks. I shall need a boy to help me who can swim. Would you be willing?'

Matthew found himself staring dizzily and stupidly at the suggestion. Could anything be more fortunate?

'I—I would like to, and I can swim,' he stammered. 'But I work at the farm, Virgin Farm up the river.'

'You've not been here long,' the man remarked. 'I can tell that by your voice. Where have you come from?'

'Gloucester.' It seemed better to be truthful for he dared not make mistakes with the shrewd stranger. He explained briefly about the journey south for the sake of the sick child. 'I am only an extra hand on the farm and Mistress Barfutt may let me go,' he finished hopefully.

'In that case I will ride up one evening and ask her. My name is Hogg, John Hogg, and I am lodging at the mill below the Priory. It would be wiser if you said nothing yourself to your mistress about my suggestion and wiser, too, if you did not come to the mill. I prefer to keep my business to myself, although the miller is reticent enough.' Master Hogg slipped his foot in the stirrup and mounted his horse.

Matthew, in a dream of excitement and pleasure, watched him ride off in the direction of Christchurch. In one brief morning he had seen the layout of the harbour, the kind of boat in use on it, the narrow mouth into the sea, and, in all probability had become the servant of Master Hogg who, whether he knew it or not, was going to aid them in their escape out of the country.

He decided that, as he had accomplished so much, there would be no harm in going farther and seeing the fishing hamlet at the harbour mouth. Leading the pony, for he did not want to go back to the road, he wandered happily across the marsh until he joined the lane which led to Mudeford. As Master Hogg had said, it was only a tiny village consisting of a few cottages clustering under the tall pines and around the little jetty at the harbour mouth. After the stillness of the marsh, the sound of wind and water was deafening and terrifying. The two rivers had made a long, narrow channel through which they swept out into the open sea, and the sea, rushing in on the tide, met the swift current in a turmoil of white spouts and tumultuous waves. On the far side was a neck of golden sand and marram grass climbing to a headland and, on the calm horizon, as though floating in the mist, was an island of shrouded cliffs and pale green hills.

'The Isle of Wight, where King Charles was kept at Carisbrooke before they brought him to London,' Matthew murmured.

It was impossible to believe that that island, trembling in the haze of early morning, was real, or that it contained people, people who lived as he did and who had shut the King in a solid castle in which the little princess Elizabeth had died, a prisoner too, only the previous summer.

It was a thought which jolted him into action. He had the miller's answer to deliver and much to discuss with Giles and Nicholas if they were to be saved from a similar fate. He sprang into the saddle, swung the pony's head away from the sea and set off at a gallop for the farm.

Sarah Barfutt was waiting impatiently for him, not that she showed her impatience, but she was hovering at the yard gate.

'Well?' she demanded as Matthew slid to the ground. 'Have you a letter for me?'

Matthew shook his head. 'He only said that he "took nothing from the cart but sacks". Those were his words.'

'Was that all?'

'He smiled,' Matthew added warily.

'Be off with you!' Mistress Barfutt's fist shot out towards Matthew's head as he ducked and ran, tugging the pony after him.

'Smiled, did he?' she muttered furiously, patting her apron over the folds of her dress. 'What has he to smile about, I should like to know?'

Chapter IX

'My Sister's Child'

IT was not the miller's lantern shining into her face that awakened Katharine the next morning, but a yellow beam of sunlight striking through the dusty panes above the bed. For a time she stared at it, puzzled by the fact that she was lying at the wrong angle in relation to the window, that it should have been shuttered and that the room should have been in darkness. Gradually she remembered what she had done, that she had run away to find Nicholas to warn him of the risks in remaining at the farm. She sprang from the mattress, only to stand uncertainly in the middle of the floor as she realized that nothing had been achieved. Nicholas and Giles were still unaware of the dangers surrounding them, Mistress Barfutt had an empty room and a guilty secret to keep, and plenty of confirmation of her suspicions, while she, herself, had betrayed to an unknown man all that Nicholas had said was to be guarded with their lives.

Katharine twisted her fingers together as the wave of doubt surged over her. In the drowsiness and security of the previous evening, the miller's story had seemed free from falsehood, now it seemed almost beyond belief. He had told her a tale of an old Master Tuck, of battles, of the mill that went on for ever, and of how he, although a Cavalier used to wealth and culture, had chosen to stay on as the miller while his friends found safety overseas.

'I don't see how he could work the mill without knowing anything about it,' she whispered. 'If only I could speak to Nicholas and tell him what I have done, at least, if it were done quickly, it might save them even now.'

She padded aimlessly round the room, her bare feet leaving

tracks in the fine film which had seeped through the cracks from the mill. As she still had no clothes, although she remembered something had been mentioned about a Mistress Tuck providing them, she dared not venture outside. Even if the miller were at work, which by the throbbing of the whole building sounded most likely, there was the merry little man who thought she was 'my sister's child' and who might be breakfasting in the room below or wandering on the stairs. It was a relief, after the first terror of being told to go to bed as if she had always lived there, to know that the miller was not willing to spread her story to anyone else.

Katharine climbed on to the bed, breathed hard on the thick, crude glass of the window and rubbed it with the edge of the blanket. The view she had then was not a wide one; a strip of cobbled yard, a strip of wooden landing-stage and blue, placid water with the sun like gold-dust glittering on its surface. Down in the corner, which she had difficulty in seeing although she squashed her nose against the pane, was the prow of a boat and someone moving, tantalizingly, almost out of her vision. The figure crossed the yard and there was a glimpse of a bright, green skirt.

'It might be Mistress Tuck,' she thought, and waited hopefully for footsteps on the stairs; but there was no sound other than the rumbling of the mill.

After a while, the green skirt returned to the boat and the prow glided out of sight. Katharine wiped the glass again where her hot breath had steamed it over, the feeling of disappointment and fear growing as the minutes passed. Then she heard someone whistling, an arm with a waving stick which struck the stones appeared under the window, a dark curly head looked up in her direction and the snub nose was unmistakable.

'Matthew, Matthew,' she hissed wildly, tapping the panes to attract his attention, but unheeding, he too went on.

When he came back in a very short time he took no notice of her window and was soon hidden from view. Katharine crouched miserably on her heels. It was possible that the miller might have told him she was there and the explanation would be passed to Nicholas, or Matthew could have been sent deliberately to learn what had happened.

Slowly, the beam of sun moved along the blanket. Tired of being shut in, tired of her grubby nightshift, feeling hungry, and chilled by the fresh autumn morning, Katharine slid from the mattress and went to the door. It was unlatched and she peeped out. Little clicking footsteps were hastening over the floors below and approaching at slackened speed up the stairs.

'Are you awake, Katharine?' a woman's voice called. 'I can see your door is open.'

Katharine darted back to the bed, feverishly wound herself in the covers and gave a muffled reply. A moment later, into the room came the owner of the bright green gown. She was small, no taller than Katharine, with grey hair showing under the white cloth of her cap; black eyes like those of a gingerbread man shone from a lined, brown face.

'I have brought you the clothes,' the woman began breathlessly. 'Poor child, I expect you thought you were never going to be dressed again.'

The 'poor child' was not said in pity, but in a light tone of amusement. Katharine leaned on her elbow and scanned with interest the colourful assortment of garments over the woman's arm. 'Are you Mistress Tuck?' she asked, shyly.

'Ay, and no one else, and I couldn't be any quicker seeing I had to row down to Mudeford and back after he told me what he wanted.' The woman dropped the clothes on the bed and sat down heavily beside them. 'I've no doubt they'll fit,' she went on. 'You're no bigger than I, maybe a shade thinner, but I can always put a stitch in the seam if they hang like sacks.'

She spread out the shift and petticoats, a faded blue gown similar to her own with a short, basqued bodice and full skirt, and a plain linen neckerchief to drape round the shoulders.

'They are clean and they are old, but they are better than nothing in the circumstances.' She smiled, showing a row of crooked, decayed teeth which might have looked grotesque in a less friendly person.

Katharine slipped to the floor and fingered the materials. They were coarser than anything she had been used to, and the cold linen shift scratched her skin as she pulled it over her head, but she felt an excitement she had never known before. Always, Hester had dressed her in white, which only accentuated her pallor. The blue of the woollen dress gave a warmth to her freckles and brought out the gold in her hazel eyes. Mistress Tuck laced up the front of the bodice and folded the neckerchief over her shoulders, pinning it low and letting the ends hang free. She combed Katharine's tangled hair, smoothing the fine strands as if it was a long sought pleasure which she was reluctant to abandon.

'Ay,' she murmured, turning her round with approval. 'You're that much taller so your skirt won't drag on the ground, but that will never matter for a child. When you have had something to eat you can look at yourself in the water by the mill—it was always the best glass, I used to think. I've no leather shoes for you to wear, you must make do with my slippers. They will be softer to your feet if they don't fit and I will find you some pattens to put on when the weather is bad.'

Katharine, so engrossed in the process of donning the unusual clothes that she had forgotten the reason for doing it, hoped fervently that the weather would remain fine. She had seen Mistress Barfutt's pattens, and was convinced that she would never be able to walk in the wooden soles raised on iron rings and fastened to the feet with straps, which kept countrywomen out of the mud. She pulled a pair of Mistress Tuck's new knitted stockings over her knees, tying on the garters to keep them in place. They were not embroidered as hers had been, but plain, solid worsted. Finally she pushed her feet into the slippers and stood up again. She took a few delighted steps and laughed, wriggling her body inside the strongly boned bodice and lifting her skirt to see the bright petticoat underneath.

'If you are ready, we had best go down,' Mistress Tuck remarked. 'I know you're supposed to be the miller's niece and as Master Hogg has gone out it should not be too hard for you at the moment.'

The reminder jolted Katharine out of her happy mood. As Nicholas had said, they were not playing a game. Gravely, she followed the widow to the living-room, which she was thankful to find was empty, and ate the food placed in front of her.

'I'll show you the rooms later and the cupboards and chests so you'll know where everything is kept. And you'd better watch what I'm doing now, for you'll have to get a meal for the men tomorrow morning,' Mistress Tuck warned her as she moved from dresser to table, table to hearth, carrying jugs, dishes, baking-pans and loaves. 'I come up every day to bake and wash and keep the floors swept, but if you're here they will expect you to work.'

Katharine stared at her in dismay. 'I don't know how to,' she faltered.

'It won't harm you to learn,' was the blunt reply. 'There was much I learnt when a girl that stood me in good stead after I was widowed. I daresay there's a deal you know more than I; music and books, like him——' Mistress Tuck glanced at the miller's shelf with its row of darkly bound volumes. 'Even if you can't handle a boat either, no doubt you can handle a horse and ride to the hunt.'

Katharine shook her head. Horses and hunting were pastimes which were not possible after her father's death.

'Much good they would have done you, anyway,' Mistress Tuck snapped. 'If it hadn't been for the love of such pleasures the King and his Cavaliers wouldn't have had to fight for their lives. You wealthy folk wouldn't dream of hunting because you were hungry, of killing a beast because your children were starving. The poor can get hanged for stealing a beast but the rich can go out, a score maybe, running a frightened animal to death, just for the enjoyment it gives them to ride and see it torn to pieces at the end. Coward's work.' The widow's dark eyes flashed contemptuously. 'Not one of them would have the wits or the cunning to tackle it alone—and folk can starve while they have their pleasure. There, I've said enough—old Tuck used to tell me my tongue would be my ruin one of these days.' She rattled the pans over the fire until her indignation was cooled and she was able to smile. 'Off you go, child, out to the water and admire yourself, while I wash the dishes.'

Katharine went, across the warm cobbles, along the landing-stage and on to the stones, where she knelt overlooking the river. The water in the little inlet was smooth as glass and as mirror-like as a polished pewter plate. It reflected the sky, the overhanging grass and Katharine in her blue dress with her fair hair falling each side of her face. Afraid that if she stayed there too long someone might see her and think she was vain, she got to her feet and wandered behind the mill. A narrow bridge with two arches spanned the swift mill stream and joined the track to the Priory grounds. By the bridge, were the remains of what might once have been a garden for the mill; the ground was damp, waterlogged through neglect, and the weeds and flowers gone wild exuberantly scattered their seeds from tall and massive stems. Behind a barrier of wizened gooseberry bushes, the miller's goat regarded Katharine with unwinking interest out of its wicked dark eyes, and she retreated hurriedly to safety.

She recognized the porch under which she had stood while waiting for the cart to be unloaded, and had the courage, now that it was daytime, to look through the door. She saw the same scene that Matthew had, with the miller bending over a sack sifting the flour between his fingers. He glanced up as her shadow blocked the light, nodded and came to speak to her.

'I see that Mistress Tuck has taken you into her hands,' he said.

As soon as she was in his presence Katharine's earlier doubts vanished, although she felt sure that when she had left him they might return again.

'She has been saying what will be expected of me if I stay, the cooking and the cleaning, and I know nothing of them,' she explained.

His answer, that there was no harm in learning, was so like Mistress Tuck's that Katharine realized that the world of the mill was very different from hers in Gloucester, where she had been spoiled and petted and the easiest path chosen for her.

'You will have to stay here, Kate,' the miller said, as if he had read her thoughts. 'You cannot go back to the farm without making some difficult explanations which will involve too many people. There is Master Hogg. He believes you are my niece, and there is no need for him to think otherwise. The fewer in a secret the safer it is, and as it is we shall have to speak very cautiously of our plans, and never in the living-room. It is too quiet, and words can run along the walls there like mice in the wainscot. The sooner your brother is able to leave the country the better for all of us, particularly as Mistress Barfutt has already tried to find out if you are here. She is apparently not prepared to tell the truth nor let it be known that you have disappeared.'

'I saw Matthew,' Katharine hesitated. 'If I could have spoken to him I would have asked him to tell Nicholas what I have done. I—I know Nicholas will think badly of me.' If he found out and she was unable to explain first, her situation at the mill would be almost as unbearable as the room at Virgin Farm. 'Could I write—about you, and say that you will help us?' she pleaded.

The miller shook his head. 'There is too much danger in

letter-writing,' he replied. He went to his bench where he had papers and a book of accounts of all the grain and meal that had passed through his hands. He turned the pages with the tip of his quill, seemingly absorbed in checking the lists. 'Letters get mislaid or blown away in the wind when they should be burnt.'

Katharine studied him anxiously. 'Could you meet Nicholas?' she ventured. 'Could you see him here or at the farm?'

The answer was a firm 'No' which startled her. 'It must be managed without that,' he added, looking at his sack which was filling up rapidly. 'No good purpose will be served by a meeting between your brother and me.'

As his work seemed to be needing his whole attention Katharine slipped away unnoticed. Puzzled, and again doubtful, she went slowly to find Mistress Tuck. It was strange that the miller wanted so much secrecy, and yet was so reluctant to make any contact with the fugitives at the farm.

Chapter X

Voyages of Discovery

HAVING left Matthew on the edge of the marsh, Master Hogg rode by the river, through Christchurch and beyond, to the bridge over the Stour and up on to the rocky headland which partly closed the harbour. It was a long way round to reach a point that had only been a few yards' distance from him at Mudeford, but there was no other means of getting across the harbour and two rivers when on horseback. Even on foot, it was not always possible to find a man willing to ferry a traveller to the other side, nor were the fords often usable after wet weather. The top of the cliff was covered in short turf and high banks of heather; behind it lay the hostile country of rolling heaths stretching towards Poole, and beneath it lay the rocks, and turbulent sea ever pounding away at the immovable barrier.

Master Hogg dismounted on the hill and led his horse, walking slowly, hat in hand, as if enjoying the warm autumn sunshine and the magnificent view he had on all sides. Out to sea lay the Isle of Wight, its cliffs still finely misted; inland, Christchurch, the Priory, the two rivers sweeping into the basin of water, lay like a coloured map at his feet. In front, the narrow gap of the salmon run, between him and Mudeford, which he had been unable to cross, looked from that height like a strip of blue ribbon. He knotted his horse's reins and let it wander loose to graze, while he selected a smooth patch of grass and settled himself comfortably on the ground. From the depths of one of his pockets he pulled several thicknesses of paper and a stub of lead pencil and, having made a firm base with his crooked knee, began to draw the scene around him.

Gradually a map took shape, until Master Hogg held in his hand the whole line of the country and coast as far as he could see—from Poole in the west, to the long bank of shingle which ran out into the Solent near Lymington. At the end of the spit stood Hurst Castle, where Charles I had been imprisoned on leaving the Isle of Wight. It was a circular fortress, bleak, lonely, well garrisoned, its empty eyes staring for ever at the changing sea and sky. He put arrows pointing to places many miles out of sight—Dorchester, Bristol, Salisbury, Southampton and Dover—and on the back of the map he wrote several headings in neat columns—*high tide, low tide, shipping, when sailing, destination.* When he had finished he slipped paper and pencil into his pocket again and remained for some time deep in thought, until a small ship, its white sails billowing, glided into the bay. He seemed disappointed when it made no attempt to approach the entrance of the harbour or to anchor off the shore, but finally disappeared like a tiny blown feather.

Suddenly, as if remembering that he had work to do, he jumped up, called his horse and retraced his steps to the bridge. This was so narrow that there was no room for two wagons to pass, and often a carter had to send a boy on ahead to warn an oncoming cart before the two met face to face in the middle. From the bridge, Master Hogg went back into Christchurch, had a poor meal at the inn, paused for a while to study the partly ruined castle and to admire the graceful windows in the Constable's house before turning his horse's head northwards in the direction of Sopley. He gave a grunt of satisfaction on reaching the stone cross by a farm on the road, because he knew he was going the right way.

At Sopley he stopped again, apparently taking pleasure in the river and the bridge and the thatched cottages covered with creeper and late roses. He enquired of a woman shaking her blankets from the window the direction of Virgin Farm and, bowing his thanks, rode on, branching away from the main track to one deeply rutted which led towards the Forest.

He viewed with interest the pastures, the girls tending the cattle and herding the sheep, and the last of the corn harvest being scythed with long, slow strokes.

He passed Mistress Barfutt's barn, allowed his horse to pick its way daintily across the muddy yard and dismounted at the open farmhouse door. He thumped with his gloved fist on the wooden panels and was ready with a friendly smile when Sarah Barfutt's frowning face, her hands covered in the dough she had been kneading, appeared to demand what he wanted.

'A few words with you, ma'am, if you are Mistress Barfutt,' he replied.

'Ay, come in, then,' she muttered. 'But I can't stop my baking, so you'll just have to sit on the settle and not mind me working while you talk.'

As Master Hogg entered, his eyes took in the whole of the tidy kitchen, the gleaming pans, the blackened pots over the fire, the herbs drying from the ceiling, and the dark-haired woman, dressed in more fashionable and expensive material, who was sewing at the side of the hearth. He bowed at her wan smile of greeting and accepted the seat she indicated before telling them both why he had come. He explained about his accidental meeting with Matthew and how he needed a boy to help him in his scheme.

'The boy had no business to be down near the harbour anyhow,' was Mistress Barfutt's sharp retort. 'He was sent to the mill. But he's not my property to hire out to you. He is one of the servants my Cousin Hester brought with her from Gloucester. I'm willing for you to have him if she is; he's nothing but impudent and lazy around the farm.'

Master Hogg glanced questioningly at Hester, who nodded her head in agreement. While she had been listening to the conversation she had seen, as Matthew had, the wonderful possibilities of escape it offered. Although she was not able at that moment to consult Giles, she felt sure that he would not mind, for with careful planning one of Master Hogg's boats, probably without his knowledge, might be used to good advantage.

'I shall need the boy tomorrow,' Master Hogg went on. 'As the farm is some distance from the town and I shall want him early, if you can provide him with the pony he had today it will be quicker than walking or hoping for a passing carter.'

'Could he not lodge at the mill, too?' Hester suggested. With Matthew at the mill on the edge of the harbour their chances of escape would be doubled. 'He could be with you at any hour, then.'

'There is scarcely the space,' Master Hog murmured doubtfully. 'The rooms are tiny and there are three of us as it is, myself, the miller and his niece.'

'Niece? I thought the miller of Place lived alone with a woman who came in to cook and clean every day,' Sarah Barfutt snapped.

'Maybe he does as a rule, but there's a child there at the moment. She was sitting by the fire eating her supper in her nightgown when I arrived last night, and he said she was his niece.'

Mistress Barfutt stopped kneading, and her arms, floury to the elbow, were poised above the board. She glanced quickly from Master Hogg to Hester, but neither appeared to think there was anything unusual in the statement. Master Hogg was trying to balance one boot on the other, by resting the tip of a spur on the toe, and Hester's head was bent over her needlework. Mistress Barfutt's mind sped back to earlier in the day when Matthew had returned with the miller's reply. 'He smiled,' the boy had said, and now it looked as though the miller had reason to be amused. She longed to question Master Hogg about the girl, but dared not because he might wonder at her interest, and Hester most certainly would. If Master Hogg described the child, Hester could not fail to recognize the description if it fitted Katharine, whom she still thought was upstairs in bed.

'I'll let the boy have the pony,' she replied, plunging her hands into the soft dough. There was a drawback she immediately realized, because if Matthew saw the girl at the mill, now that he knew she was supposed to have the smallpox, it could set in motion a series of events with far-reaching results. 'Do you want him at the mill in the morning?' she asked aloud.

'I will meet him at the Staple Cross outside Christchurch,' Master Hogg replied.

As if pleased with his answer, Mistress Barfutt left her dough and fetched refreshment for her guest, ale and cheesecakes, which she placed on a stool at his side.

'I see you are a widow, ma'am,' Master Hogg began, taking a drink of ale. 'Do you run the farm alone?'

'Ay, and have done these ten years.' Mistress Barfutt was proud of the fact and always willing to talk of her work.

'You must have many hands, then, men and girls to help you?'

'A good number,' she replied.

Master Hogg looked through the open door to where Giles, muck-rake in hand, had paused on the other side of the yard.

'That fellow is strong enough by the look of him,' he remarked.

'Ay, but he is none of mine. He belongs to my cousin.'

'I see, one of the servants you brought with you from Gloucester?' His lips smiled upon Hester, but his eyes studied the swarthy figure.

Hester smiled back at him. 'The roads are lonely even during the day and swarming with footpads. I travelled with the strongest, other than the boy, who could give me most protection.' That explanation was the answer she had had in readiness all along the route.

Master Hogg nodded silently, finished his ale and cakes, bowed good-bye and went out to mount his horse.

As soon as he had gone, Mistress Barfutt covered her dough with a cloth and set it to rise near the oven, and explaining to her cousin that she was going to visit a neighbour for a few hours and that the dairymaids could manage on their own for the evening, she hurried outside to the stable. As she went she tied a large scarf over her head to prevent the ends of her cap from flying in her face. In the stable she harnessed a pony to the little cart which she normally used for taking her vegetables and farm produce to market, and then drove through the yard gate. She was glad to see Master Hogg's round shape astride his horse which was ambling in the direction of Ringwood. She flicked the pony's neck with her whip and trotted in the opposite direction, to Christchurch. While finishing her bread she had decided that she would have to visit Place Mill herself and find out if Katharine were there. If she were, she would have to handle the ensuing situation with subtlety.

The mill was still working when she reached it, which meant that, for a time at least, the miller would be occupied and his niece probably alone. She stopped the pony and left the cart several yards below the bridge, going on foot with her usual soft stealth to the worn steps leading into the living-room. A girl in a blue dress was standing at the table, cutting thick slices from a loaf of brown bread.

'Aha, so there you are,' said Mistress Barfutt's bantering voice.

Katharine dropped the knife and clutched the bread between her hands. 'Mistress Barfutt,' she whispered, as the solid figure moved noiselessly into the room.

'I thought I should find you here,' the widow remarked pleasantly and, not taking any more notice of Katharine, began to show a lively interest in the miller's room. 'Books,' she murmured, touching the volumes on the shelf. 'Pewter on the dresser, a fine oak table and settle.' She ran her fingers over the surface of the wood and out of habit turned them up to see if they were covered in dust. 'These were not the property of old Miller Tuck, that I know. He's a man of learning is this new miller—and was that why you came to visit him, child?' she asked abruptly, facing the frightened girl.

'You know why I came, because you were starving me and I was hungry,' Katharine faltered.

'There was no need to come here for food if you were that hungry, there was plenty in the kitchen at Virgin.'

'I did not know what to do—I ran out into the yard.' It did not matter what she said so long as Mistress Barfutt did not discover the real reason why she had left.

'And why hide in the cart that was coming to the mill?'

'I did not know it was coming here, I heard you in the yard and hid among the sacks so that you would not see me, and when you had gone I was going back to my room.'

'A likely story,' Mistress Barfutt muttered contemptuously. 'And when you got to the mill, I suppose the miller was not surprised to see you, and just unloaded you with the sacks?'

'No, he told me to get down and wait in the porch.'

'Tiddly, widdly, whatever next! He never thought of calling for Barney and sending you straight home?'

Katharine shook her head.

Mistress Barfutt laughed. 'No, because he had sent Barney indoors to drink his health, no doubt because he had expected to find you there.'

'I don't understand you,' Katharine murmured, growing more uneasy.

'He was ready enough to pass you off as his niece when someone came knocking at the door. Or was Master Hogg well prepared to accept you as the miller's niece, eh?'

'Master Hogg had nothing to do with it, he wanted a lodging.'

'There's an inn in the town. Why come down here past all the other houses, past the old Priory that's supposed to be haunted, to a mill and ask for a night's lodging?'

Katharine was unable to reply. She crumbled the crust of the loaf, scattering little pieces on the floor.

'I shall go home now,' Mistress Barfutt announced.

'M-may I fetch the miller?' Katharine asked quickly.

'I've no wish to meet that impudent fellow,' was the brisk reply. 'I shall go home,' she continued slowly. 'I shall go home and tell your Cousin Hester where you are, and I shall also tell her — ' she checked with a gesture Katharine's move of protest — 'I shall tell her that you ran away and that I, stupid woman that I was, pretended you had the smallpox because I hadn't the courage to confess that you had disappeared.'

'That — that's a lie,' Katharine whispered.

Mistress Barfutt nodded gravely. 'Who is to know? I wonder what Cousin Hester will do when she hears you are not at the farm. Will she be upset or will she smile, having known all the time?'

'What are you trying to say? You mean something I don't understand,' Katharine cried in bewilderment.

Mistress Barfutt did not answer. She went through the door and descended the stairs, a cloud of dust following in her wake as her skirt swept the ground.

Katharine dropped the bread on the table and darted after her. Mistress Tuck had gone and there was only the miller to whom she could turn, but, at the corner of the mill as she reached it, stood Master Hogg, bowing affably to both of them and putting a stop to further conversation with anyone. Mistress Barfutt returned his greeting, passed him and climbed into the cart. This time she did not use her whip, but let the pony wander at its own speed.

She had plenty to think about on that journey home, for she felt she had almost solved a mystery. It was plain that Katharine's running away to the mill had all been part of a pre-arranged plan. Someone, as yet she could not see who, had wanted Hester to come to Virgin Farm because it was no great distance from the sea; the child had to be ill to allow for more servants than was really necessary — she had suspected the servants all along especially the black-haired Giles, though he had given no cause for suspicion either in his speech or behaviour. Why had Katharine gone to the mill? To contact the miller, perhaps, but Matthew was in a very good position to do that.

As the cart trundled along the rough road Mistress Barfutt's brain, so used to working out her farm accounts, struggled with the equally difficult problem. It was a very involved plot, of that she was certain, and if so involved it would surely be in aid of an important person, hardly the child's brother as she had first thought. Why not the King? She was convinced it was the King and her mind flew once more to the one thousand pounds. The three servants, Katharine, Cousin Hester, the miller, and now Master Hogg with his sudden interest in her farm workers, were all striving together for Charles Stuart's escape. And would it not be possible for one of them to be Charles Stuart?

The whip touched the pony's shoulder in Mistress Barfutt's sudden agitation and the cart leaped forward, swaying violently over the ruts. 'Steady, Sarah,' she whispered to herself. 'This is where you must be careful, and there's not much time. One hint to any of them that you are suspicious and they'll be gone like a flock of frightened sheep. If only I knew what the King really looked like—he can't be that man Giles.' The difficulties for a royal prince acting the part of a servant for any length of time seemed insurmountable. 'I'll send up to Ringwood or Winchester to the soldiers there, and as I shall not get a reply for some days I must bait my hook well.'

Satisfied with her afternoon's work and with her plans neatly laid, Mistress Barfutt calmed the pony, fastened her scarf tidily over her head again and trotted home to Virgin Farm.

Chapter XI

A Night Visitor

'BUT it is impossible, I just cannot believe it.' Giles flung himself on his mattress in the loft, clasped his hands behind his head and stared at his friend.

Nicholas, cross-legged like a tailor, needle and thread in his fingers, was stitching carefully at his frayed coat.

'I saw Hester only a short while ago,' he repeated. 'She was feeding the hens and made the excuse that the bucket was too heavy so that I would carry it for her and be able to talk. Unless we invent some kind of story, there is no opportunity for learning what is going on. She told me that her Cousin Barfutt went to Place Mill yesterday and saw Kate for herself. Apparently there was nothing wrong with the child at all—the stupid woman discovered she had run away and was too frightened to tell Hester, so she pretended the child had the smallpox so that Hester would not go near the room.'

'But why? Why did she do it? Why go to the mill?' Giles asked in exasperation. 'She knew our hopes depended on her. When I carried her upstairs she was quite prepared to go through with our plan.'

Nicholas shrugged his shoulders. 'Why does Kate do anything? She did not want to come originally, she did not want to pretend to be ill, and I suppose she made up her mind that she was not going to stay in bed until we gave her permission to get better, even though I warned her of the consequences to us.'

'But how did Mistress Barfutt know she was at the mill?' Giles persisted.

'Master Hogg told her—the little man that Matthew was

fortunate enough to meet. I don't think he realizes who she is, I hope not, or where she has come from. He believes she is the miller's niece.'

'Who told him that?'

'The miller.'

'The miller!' Giles exclaimed in astonishment. 'Why should he? Why didn't he send her back to the farm?'

'I do not know,' Nicholas replied heavily. 'I do not know the answers to any of these questions, nor to the hundreds I should like to ask. All I know is that Kate has behaved despicably. She would rather we were dead than be uncomfortable herself.'

'I don't believe it, Nick,' Giles muttered. 'You have not seen her for years and you can hardly know her.'

'Have you been so impressed by what you have seen?' Nicholas asked sharply. 'We were tempted to mistrust Mistress Barfutt when Matthew said he had seen Kate in the barn, but this has proved us wrong. She ran away because she could put up with the discomfort no longer, and as Mistress Barfutt has been telling the truth all the time, I, for one, am quite ready to confide in her and ask if she will give us any help.'

Giles sat up quickly. 'No,' he said decidedly, 'I am not prepared to do that. Has she asked why Katharine ran away when she was really supposed to be suffering from the effects of the litter? Has she asked why Katharine is masquerading as the niece of a miller who is willing to accept her as such? Mistress Barfutt is no fool, Nicholas; she has kept a big farm without advice from a man for ten years, which shows she has a shrewd head on her shoulders. If she is not asking herself as many questions as we are asking each other, then I'm ——' He broke off suddenly as there was a noise in the barn below.

The ladder leading into the loft quivered, and Matthew appeared through the trap-door in the floor. His pockets were bulging with fruit.

'From Dame Barfutt,' he announced cheerfully, emptying it on to the floor. 'She seemed pleased, patted me on the head and said I was a good lad for not overtiring the pony.'

Giles glanced significantly at Nicholas, who pretended not to notice and helped himself to a pear. He began to tell Matthew of the further news of Katharine.

'I was sure she had climbed into one of the carts,' Matthew agreed. 'Master Hogg mentioned a girl being at the mill today. He said she was so quiet that he called her Mistress Mouse.'

'A description that would fit Kate admirably,' Nicholas muttered. 'Though why she should choose to have a miller as her uncle is beyond me. What game is the child playing at?' he exclaimed, flinging his coat across the loft and stabbing the needle savagely into the beam at his side. 'Ever since we left Gloucester we have done nothing but worry about Kate and say our lives depended on her. Certainly our lives will be forfeit if we stay here much longer. It is time we concentrated on the reason why we are here and found a means of leaving the country. We must forget her—she has chosen to fend for herself and three lives cannot be risked for one. She seems safe enough where she is.'

'Very well,' Giles nodded. 'She is your sister and if you feel she is no longer your responsibility, that is nothing to do with me, although I will say this: if the opportunity occurs for us to escape, you ought to see her before you leave. Whatever your feelings for her at the moment, that surely, is only your duty.'

Nicholas frowned. 'Hester will be here. It will not be necessary, and when I have gone they can return to Gloucester together.' With a swift change of subject he turned to ask Matthew about his day's work with Master Hogg.

Matthew had enjoyed himself, and now he was enjoying even more the fact that Giles and Nicholas were watching him with interest and waiting to hear all that he had done. He struck a light and kindled the lantern, setting it so that its glow fell on their faces, chose an apple from the pile and, with suppressed excitement, began his story.

He had met Master Hogg at the Staple Cross. They had ridden to the harbour, where he had rowed his new master to several of the small boats anchored there, although the wind and tide coming in from the sea had been almost too strong for him. They had spoken to the master of a coasting vessel, which was carrying a cargo of barley-meal to Portsmouth. He had told them when he was sailing, that there were a number of sailings of coasters carrying rushes, malt and flour from Christchurch to Portsmouth and Fareham, and a few bringing in goods, mainly wheat to be milled. All of which Master Hogg noted down on a piece of paper. After that, they made enquiries about the tides and found that there were four tides daily, an unusual number owing to the ebb from the Solent which made an extra high tide about two hours after the first. Master Hogg seemed particularly pleased with this discovery and wrote down the times with special reference to the harbour mouth. He was disappointed on hearing how shallow the water was in the harbour, barely more than five feet in places, and so changeable that it needed men who knew it thoroughly to navigate boats of any draught.

'If we could approach the master of one of these ships,' Giles interrupted, 'bribe him, giving some reason, not the real one, to sail apparently for Portsmouth but make a detour to drop us off the French coast, and then return with his cargo, no one need be any the wiser that he had gone elsewhere first.'

'It would be a risky run through the Solent,' Nicholas commented. 'It would have to be a very sympathetic seaman and he would probably want a substantial bribe before he would agree to anything so foolhardy.'

'That is where Master Hogg will be able to help,' Matthew broke in.

'Master Hogg, at the moment, scarcely knows the seamen any better than we do, and we know nothing of Master Hogg,'

Giles warned him. 'It will take time and it will be like groping in the dark; one false step and we all, including Hester, who you must remember is a Catholic and therefore suspect, will find ourselves behind bars or on the way to the gallows.'

'It seems to me,' Nicholas said, 'that there are two possible people who might help us, Master Hogg and Mistress Barfutt. We know most about Mistress Barfutt, who seems honest although you, Giles, for no definite reason, view her with mistrust. We are not to know if she accepted Kate's disappearance without question nor would she tell us if she felt any concern.'

Matthew wrinkled his nose in the manner Katharine had found so annoying. He disliked Mistress Barfutt and had no wish to be assisted by her. He preferred Master Hogg, whom he had found exceptionally pleasant and easy to work for. Mistress Barfutt had taken it for granted that he would try to shirk any task she gave him, and she had been very free with her fists. On the other hand, Master Hogg was jovial, good-tempered and had even found the time during their busy day to point out to the ignorant Matthew some of the water-birds on the marshes. Matthew buried his teeth in the crisp, white flesh of his apple, thoughts of the widow uppermost in his mind. Suddenly, he stopped in the middle of a bite.

'I am sure,' he said slowly, 'that Mistress Barfutt told your cousin, Nicholas, that Katharine had the smallpox *before* I saw her in the barn. Cousin Hester told you much later, but I believe she said that Mistress Barfutt thought Katharine was sickening for the smallpox on the day we arrived. Katharine could hardly have run away by then.'

The atmosphere was tense, the lantern burned steadily and there were strange rustlings and tappings from within the walls.'

'You think Mistress Barfutt is lying?' Giles suggested.

Matthew looked uncomfortable at the blunt statement, and waited for his brother to go on.

'If she is, why say Kate was ill in the first instance? Why the smallpox? Why begin to lie so soon after our arrival?'

Matthew shook his head. The noises in the wall became more audible.

'It's not mice or beetles,' Nicholas whispered as the three stared at each other. 'Someone is walking through the barn underneath us.' He crawled stealthily to the trap. 'Give me the lantern, I am going down.'

There was silence, while he and the light descended the

ladder. When he reached the bottom he swung the lantern aloft and its beam swayed over the stalls. At the side of one stood a small, slight figure.

'Katharine! ' Nicholas exclaimed, and started forward.

'I am not Katharine,' the figure whispered hurriedly. 'I have come from where she is, from the mill, to speak with her brother.'

Nicholas drew back at the sight of the frail, elderly woman, her head and shoulders swathed in a large woollen shawl.

'I am Katharine's brother,' he replied sternly, angered that this complete stranger should be aware of the relationship which they had hidden so well.

'She is safe at the mill and unharmed,' the woman continued breathlessly in a nervous voice. She kept glancing into the yard as if afraid that someone might see her. 'The miller knows about you and will help—you must trust him—he would not write, letters are dangerous, and he cannot come. Have no dealings with the widow Barfutt, she already suspects the child and your journey here——' The woman turned towards the door and Nicholas, thinking she was leaving, barred the way.

'This is mad,' he exclaimed. 'You come out of the night from nowhere and expect me to put my life into the hands of someone I have never heard of, who gives no reason for his willingness to help, other than the fact that my sister is safe with him at the mill. She should never have gone there. What has she told him about me?'

'Enough,' the woman replied simply, 'for him to risk his own life for the three of you. Now let me pass, I came up from Mudeford and if the tide has turned by the time I reach the bridge I shall not have the strength to row through the harbour.'

Although so shabby and small, there was a dignity about her which made Nicholas ashamed of his brusque manner. He stood to one side and, like a grey shadow, she slipped out into the darkness. He pulled the barn door after her and fastened it with the wooden bolt.

At the top of the ladder, when he climbed slowly up again, Giles and Matthew were waiting. 'You heard everything?' he queried.

They nodded and Giles took the lantern from his friend's trembling fingers, fingers that were shaking with fury because of his sister's indiscretion.

'She must have told him all she could.' Nicholas was unable to control himself any longer and paced the loft with heavy steps. 'She has acted so that Sarah Barfutt suspected us from the first; probably on finding that the widow was suspicious, Kate realized what she had done and ran away; somehow, she gets taken to the mill. She probably hid in the cart and fell asleep and when she arrived at the mill, she was so frightened that she blurted out to thc man the whole story——'

'Nevertheless,' Giles began carefully, not wanting to add fuel to the fire of Nicholas's temper, 'she has not done us any real harm, if the man is prepared to help.'

'But is he?' Nicholas stopped in his walk and swung round to face them both. 'How do we know that this is not some plot of the miller's to get us into his hands and then betray us to the soldiers? It would make a fine catch for a poor miller, five of us, with probably an ample reward from the authorities. Why cannot he write? Why not come himself instead of sending a message by an old woman who could scarcely remember it and was wanting to be off again as soon as she was here? I will not trust either of them, either this miller or Sarah Barfutt.'

'He warned us about her,' Matthew murmured.

'Yes,' Nicholas agreed, 'and if it were at all possible I should like to leave this farm tomorrow. Mistress Barfutt suspects Hester's reason for coming, the miller knows everything, and I should be a great deal happier if neither of them knew where to find us.'

Giles was lying flat on his back, staring at the rafters and the cobwebs above his head. In the dim lantern light they looked mysterious, netted with dead leaves, twists of straw and pale wraiths of moths—a fate which could be their own if they were not prepared to come to a quick decision.

'We are left with Master Hogg,' he said gravely. 'I suggest that we make a plan, and one of us meets him and puts the proposal to him that he finds us a ship willing, for a reason not as yet specified, to take us to France.'

Nicholas sat down, burying his face in his hands. 'We are almost accepting his loyalty without any test,' he objected.

Giles laughed. 'The other alternative is to swim.'

The atmosphere was eased and Nicholas settled himself on his mattress preparing to talk far into the night. Matthew, stretched on his pallet, knew that in spite of his interest in the scheme he would not be able to keep awake much longer. He listened drowsily for a few minutes, until worn out with the strenuous day, he fell asleep.

Giles outlined to Nicholas the plan he had in mind. In order for them to slip out of the country secretly they would have to give a valid reason to anyone who was helping them, and it would have to be a reason that would not involve that helper too deeply if caught. It was no use saying they were Royalists and expecting the master of a vessel to be sympathetic. The reward for their capture by the authorities might be greater than the bribe they could offer, and the punishment for helping fugitives could, in many cases, be severe.

'We must expect to pay something in the region of fifty or sixty pounds,' Giles said.

Nicholas expressed surprise. 'If Hester has not that amount with her, I do not know who has. We are both penniless,' he exclaimed. 'Unless Master Hogg carries his wealth with him—merchants are usually rich. What reason are we to give for needing a ship?' he asked.

'We can either say we are a pair of runaway lovers, in which case Matthew will have to dress as a woman, as he is the smallest, while we are nobleman and servant. Or we can have taken part in a fatal duel and be fleeing to escape the consequences. Matthew can be a servant or younger brother, either would pass.'

'I cannot see Matthew taking readily to your first idea,' Nicholas observed. 'It would be more difficult to find the disguise, too. As we are, we look more like your last suggestion. Which of us will approach Master Hogg?'

'I will, after Matthew has paved the way with part of the story and asked if it is possible for a meeting to be arranged. Master Hogg has seen neither of us, and he need not know where we are hiding. I will make up a convincing tale for Matthew to tell him, of how he met us at an inn on the way down — we might have stopped the horses from bolting, perhaps — he has met us again here, and would like to repay our former kindness by giving us some assistance. Now, his acquaintanceship with Master Hogg seems to have made this more possible.'

Nicholas nodded slowly. 'It sounds practicable,' he agreed, 'even when invented at that speed, and when it has been worked out more thoroughly, it should be foolproof.' He yawned, and pulling off his shoes, rolled on his side for a few hours' sleep before the day's labour started at dawn.

Giles extinguished the candle. As soon as the glow had died away, the barn was filled with all the tiny sounds which could only be heard at night. The creaks as the warm beams cooled, a mouse trailing an ear of wheat the length of the loft, and the moths, lost without the light to dance in, fluttering against the shuttered lantern.

Giles did not close his eyes for some time. He stared into the darkness, turning over his plan in his mind, examining the flaws, polishing the story Matthew would have to tell to the merchant, and the words he would use at his own meeting with Master Hogg. He wondered about Katharine at the mill, and what could have driven her away from the farm to jeopardize their safety so thoughtlessly. Although he would not admit it to Nicholas, he was disappointed in the girl. But was it only selfishness on her part, or was it something more sinister, to do with Mistress Barfutt, who had apparently woven such a web of lies about the smallpox?

Chapter XII

Master Hogg's Map

KATHARINE found that one of the easiest tasks allotted to her by Mistress Tuck was the cleaning of the rooms. The floor of the living-room was stone and because of the constant dust from the mill was kept bare of rushes or other covering. It was simple work to run the broom under the table and settle, gather the heaped dust together and toss it in the river. Katharine usually left the tidying of the bookshelf until last, when she felt she had accomplished her other work and could take the heavy volumes into her lap, finger the worn bindings and read the black printed pages. There were Walter Raleigh's *History of the World* which she had known at home, poetry by Edmund Spenser and a *Herball* by a man called John Gerard, particularly interesting because it had woodcuts of all the plants, and there were several books with Latin titles. She could not help wondering if the miller were wise to show his knowledge so openly, especially as Mistress Barfutt's quick eye had immediately noticed it. On the other hand, she remembered Hester telling her once of a local squire who bought all the freshly published books to adorn his new library and had scarcely opened one of them, certainly not to read. The miller could be the same and his books would not arouse suspicion unless suspicion were there already.

On the day after Mistress Barfutt's visit, Katharine, half afraid that the widow might appear again, spent most of her time until Mistress Tuck's arrival sweeping upstairs. Her own room, now that the bed had been provided with sheets and a coloured counterpane, was more comfortable than it had been before. She took great pleasure in rubbing the dirty window, brushing cobwebs from the rafters and placing the two stools, one to hold jug, basin and ball of soap, and the other for her candlestick, where they would be most convenient. The boarded floor was so rotten with wood-worm, that after it had been swept there were loose pieces of wood mixed with the dust. Katharine thought it wiser to replace them, for it seemed more sensible to have cracked boards than an uneven floor full of holes.

Having finished there, she went down the short flight of stairs to the narrow landing, where there were two other rooms, those of Master Hogg and the miller. Knowing that the merchant was out, she pushed open his door and went in.

As Master Hogg had told Mistress Barfutt, his room was very tiny. There was only space for the bed against the wall, head under the window, with a stool at the side on which he had his Bible, a candlestick, and a rushlight as well. The last, Katharine noticed with amazement at his extravagance, he had been burning at both ends. Apparently he liked plenty of light after dark, when other people had gone to sleep.

Katharine was determined to remain out of the living-room for as long as possible, thereby avoiding any unexpected visitors, and so, with the enthusiasm of someone new to the work, she began to clean Master Hogg's room as if it had never before been touched. Eagerly, she pulled all the blankets from the bed and dropped them on the floor, she thumped the heavy mattress, sending dust and feathers flying into the air; she took the sheets, blankets and coverlet, one by one, and shook them vigorously out of the window, where the loose feathers got caught by the wind and went soaring away like thistledown over the river and marsh. She tugged the bed from the wall, climbed on to it and dipped her broom behind, scraping it along the wainscoting. The bristles skidded, as if unable to take a grip on the boards and she had to lean over to peer into the gap to see what was the matter.

She soon saw that the broom was sliding on a long, folded piece of thick paper. She picked it up and blew the dust from its dirty surface, realizing as she did so that it could not have been there long, because it seemed that it was only the pressure from her broom which had made the grubby streaks and nearly obliterated some of the writing. Katharine spread the paper on her knee, and knowing that it was not a letter and therefore not necessarily private, she glanced along the smudgy sheet. The writing was in pencil, in columns, headed: *high tide, low tide, shipping, when sailing* and *destination.* There were figures like times in some columns, in others names of boats and places like Portsmouth. At the bottom of the sheet was a faintly scribbled sentence, as if jotted down in a hurry as an aid to memory—'last heard Charmouth—22nd—lost London road—servant or woman—small ports, possibly here; Sept. early Oct?'

Katharine let the broom slide down at her side; the heap of bedclothes was forgotten as she curled on the mattress and studied with interest Master Hogg's puzzle. It must belong to him, of that she was sure, and he had probably been scribbling it in bed—that would account for the use of the rushlight—and when he had gone to sleep it had fallen on to the floor. Master Hogg had said he was a merchant, and the columns were the sort of thing that would be of importance to a merchant, all except the last sentence. What had Master Hogg lost on the London road on the 22nd, that was last heard of at Charmouth? Was it a servant or a woman and why did not he know? Where was Charmouth? Katharine asked herself a number of questions. Was he expecting the lost object to turn up at Christchurch in September or early October? It seemed that it could be a bundle of merchandise travelling by road, but what the servant or woman had to do with it she could not imagine.

She turned the paper over and gave an exclamation of delight. On the other side was a map, a map which she gradually began to recognize. There were the mill, the Priory, the harbour, Mudeford hamlet, where lived Mistress Tuck; roads to Lymington, to Poole, tiny cottages and trees, a vague out-

line for Virgin Farm and arrows to towns and cities off the map's area. Katharine gazed at it in admiration. If she saw Master Hogg in the evening she would ask him to tell her about it. She wriggled from the bed and propped the map against the candlestick, wedged by the rushlight holder, on the stool, where it would be noticed immediately he opened the door. Then, on hearing Mistress Tuck calling from below, she found that her eagerness to clean the room had gone. The clothes were tossed on to the mattress and hurriedly smoothed, and the little pile of dust already collected was pushed in the corner behind the door to await the sweeping of another day.

'I have brought some fish for the midday meal,' Mistress Tuck said as Katharine entered the living-room. 'Salmon, straight from the river.'

Katharine was glad she was told what it was, for to her all fish looked alike, wet, shining and glassy-eyed.

'I'll clean it and chop it into cutlets,' the widow went on, 'for I doubt whether you'll like handling raw fish as yet. You can crumble up some bread from the stale loaf and prepare the pans for the oven, and after that I'll show you what to do with the apples. There's plenty of crumbs already baked in the jar on the dresser.'

Katharine helped slowly. The fresh crumbs were put in the oven to crisp; the fish was rolled in the deep golden ones on the board, and, following the instructions, she cut the apples. They were halved, cored and pressed together again with a huge spoonful of honey inside, placed in a shallow pan of water and set in the oven beside the fire.

'I have seen your brother,' Mistress Tuck said quietly as they worked. 'I went to the farm last night with a message from the miller.'

Katharine turned towards her, breathless and eager. 'What did he say?' she asked.

'There wasn't time for much. Sarah Barfutt was prowling round the yard and I was that frightened she would see me I dared not stay long. He was none too pleased I knew who he was and none too ready to be helped by the miller, and that was not to be wondered at. I warned him about Barfutt, and said you were safe, but I told the miller myself that he would have to make it plainer than that. He says he won't have letters with well-known names flying about the farm, although I said it could go by word of mouth as the last one did.'

'Why is he afraid to tell them?' Katharine asked. 'Who—who is he—the miller?'

Mistress Tuck looked at her sharply. 'If he's not told you, neither will I,' she replied. 'I'm no gossip like some, always prying into my neighbour's business, poking my head out of the window to see what's on the washing-line, and nothing to talk of but my aches and ailments. Maybe he thinks it best you shouldn't know—there's no temptation to pass it on then.'

Katharine flushed. She had passed on to the miller so readily, even before she knew him, so much about Giles and Nicholas, that she was not surprised he was careful of what he disclosed to her.

'He's never said to me why he's such a liking for you, and it's something more than because you've a brother loyal to the King up at Virgin,' Mistress Tuck continued. 'But that's nothing to do with me. What I do know is that he is coming down to Mudeford to-night. I've a loft that runs the length of my cottage and it may do for your brother and his friend to hide in for a few days. We must decide first how we're to get them to sea, for there'll be the devil to pay when Barfutt finds they've gone from the farm. I hope your Cousin Hester is willing to take the risk, for Barfutt could have her arrested for being a papist and likely to have her finger in any Royalist pie.'

'Not her own cousin?' Katharine said in amazement.

'Why not? You told me what she said about your brother and the money for the King. If she wants a new barn and a bigger dairy she'd as good as sell her soul.'

Remembering Mistress Barfutt's treatment of herself, Katharine came to the same conclusion.

Later in the day, when Mistress Tuck had returned to Mudeford, Katharine, still uneasy at being left alone in the living-room, went into the mill for the company of the cats, if the miller were too busy to talk to her. She climbed the stairs to the top floor, where the grain was stored in hutches and where the rope pulley, used to hoist the sacks from ground level, came up through the boards and the great shaft turned with the movement of the wheel below. As she looked out of the window and saw the water patterned with the shadows of the clouds and the rushes bent in the wind, she thought of Master Hogg's map. Wondering whether to mention it to the miller, she went down to the middle floor, where the huge grindstones lay. The grain trickled evenly from the hutches above, through the hopper and into the eye of the top stone.

'That is the runner,' the miller said in answer to her query, 'because it moves and the bed-stone at the bottom keeps still.'

Katharine watched the grain gradually being worked outwards to the edge of the stones, where it poured into the open sacks in the room underneath.

'How do you stop the stones when there is no more grain?' she asked.

'Take one of the staves out of the small wheel below so that it can't catch on the cogs any longer,' the miller replied, smiling at her curiosity. 'And when I want to stop the water-wheel for the day I have to go outside to the stream and drop the hatch which cuts off the supply of water to the mill-race. Sometimes, when the river is high, I've known it trickle through and start the wheel up again. That sound is enough to wake any miller in the dead of night.'

Katharine rested her chin on the narrow sill. She felt as contented at that moment as one of the miller's three cats, who were all curled in the various warm patches of light in the room. She heard the miller leave the stones and come to stand behind her, looking over her shoulder out of the window.

'Kate,' he said, as quietly as possible above the steady rumbling, 'I have had news of the King. You need have no fears for Giles—he may be like him, but the real King was last heard of at a little fishing village in Dorset—Charmouth was its name.'

Katharine started. She had seen the word 'Charmouth' only that morning, in blurred handwriting on the back of Master Hogg's map.

'His friends had him disguised as their servant,' the miller went on, 'and they had arranged for a boat to pick him up at night. Unfortunately, the owner of the boat did not turn up—someone said he was locked in his room by his wife, who had guessed what he was hoping to do, and knew the penalty for assisting the King. In the morning, when they decided it was not safe to wait any longer, the King rode on ahead with two of his friends, while the others took a horse to the smithy. The smith nearly discovered who they were, because he recognized the nails in the horse-shoes as having been put in in the north, and the ostler said the horses had been saddled up all night, and so between them they went off to ask the parson's advice. They soon had a troop of horse in pursuit, but by good fortune, they lost track of the fugitives and, I hope, have not yet found them.'

'Lost on the London road,' Katharine thought, as she remembered Master Hogg's grubby piece of paper. So, the King was Master Hogg's mislaid merchandise, and he had known that he might be disguised as a servant. She kept her face hidden by her hands in order to cover her guilty cheeks, for she was sure that neither of the men would be pleased to know that she had discovered so much about them.

'Would the King come here, to Christchurch, for a boat?' she asked, thinking of the queried September and October.

'Here?' the miller sounded surprised. 'What makes you suggest that? I know nothing of him; the news was given to me by a carter this morning, and he heard it from an ostler. It may not all be true. But I very much doubt whether even those closest to the King know what the next step will be.' He spoke abruptly as though he did not wish to continue with the subject.

Katharine frowned, because Master Hogg seemed to have a good idea of what the next step could be, and to have known what had already happened before the miller had. Unless the miller, by his sharp tone, had been covering a mistake, and was annoyed because she had mentioned Christchurch as the next port for escape.

'Not a word of this is to be told to anyone,' the miller warned her, 'not even to Mistress Tuck. I have only told you because I hoped it would ease your mind about Giles.'

That remark made Katharine more uncomfortable than ever, for it had been on the tip of her tongue to speak of Master Hogg's map; but, she thought, perhaps Master Hogg would not be pleased if she passed on his information to the miller. Adults were odd in what they allowed to be revealed to others; sometimes everything, sometimes nothing, and sometimes scraps of news, half truths and implications which seemed to serve their strange purposes better.

Resolved to keep silent, she curled herself on one of the wooden cages which were often put over the grindstones to prevent the flour from flying about, and stayed for the remainder of the afternoon, watching the miller at his work. When she was not thinking of Hester, or Nicholas, or the secrets of the two men, she was happy and at peace. As Mistress Tuck had said, there was a security about the mill, a feeling of safety about the everlasting flow of the water, the clacking of the wheel and the rattling of the hopper as it jerked the grain to the stones. She liked the smell and the soft dust which floated in the air and settled on her dress and arms even while she sat there—and, above all, she liked the miller. He was often abrupt, and she could not always understand him, but there was a quality about him which reminded her of her father—not the wan, preoccupied man of the last few weeks of his life—but the ideal, which she still carried in her mind.

When the day's work was ended and the hatch had been dropped in the penstock across the stream, Katharine and the miller had their evening meal alone. Master Hogg was still absent on his own business. She sat by the miller's side, elbows on the table, while he talked of his books and showed marked passages to her. Now and again, he forgot that she was there, absent-mindedly turning the pages and reading to himself the Latin which she could not follow, until his long finger had traced the last line and he was conscious of the candle fluttering in her light breath. At length, he pushed back his chair and reluctantly closed the volume.

'I must go to Mudeford, Mistress Mouse,' he said quietly.

Katharine smiled, for the name, in mockery of her timidity, had remained, to be used as a term of endearment by both men. The miller had to appear affectionate towards his niece, and Master Hogg liked to tease.

The miller stood up, lifted his jacket from the back of the settle and went outside to the landing-stage. Katharine watched him unfasten his boat and row away in the darkness until she could only see his lantern bobbing on the inky water. She returned indoors, unwilling to leave the fire for the little room upstairs, and knelt by the hearth, listening to the bumps and squeaks of the cats in the mill and the gurgle of the overflow from the mill-stream. She was glad when hoofs clattered on to the cobbles and Master Hogg's voice rang out as he talked to his horse. There was a pause while he stabled and attended to the animal, and then he entered the room.

'All alone, Mistress Mouse?' he asked cheerfully, tossing his hat and gloves on the settle and warming his hands at the fire. 'The nights are getting colder, we shall have a frost soon. Take yourself off to bed, child, you must be tired. Where is my friend, the miller?'

Katharine gave the answer that the miller had suggested, 'Fishing', and Master Hogg raised his eyebrows as if he thought 'poaching' would be a better word. Then, taking her candle, she bade him 'Good night' and crept up the stairs to bed. She heard him follow and go into his room. Suddenly, there was a roar which shook the mill.

'Katharine!'

Katharine flew to her door. 'I am here,' she called.

Master Hogg marched to the foot of her stairs, and in his hand he held the map.

'Who found this?' he asked angrily.

'I did—it—it was under your bed—when I was sweeping,' she stammered.

'Did you show anyone, or tell them?' Master Hogg put his boot on the lowest step.

Katharine retreated. 'N-no,' she replied, trembling at his wrath.

He saw her fear and his manner changed immediately.

'Well, well, never mind, it would not have mattered if you had. But,' he waggled his finger, half seriously, 'this must be a secret, which we shall not tell to either Master Miller or to Mistress Tuck. We will keep it between ourselves. Do you think you can keep a secret, child?'

At Katharine's whispered 'yes', he went down and shut himself in the living-room.

Katharine shut her own door and undressed slowly. It seemed she was to be the holder of many secrets. But Master Hogg had been angry, although he had tried to hide it afterwards. It was strange, that both he and the miller should be working for the same ends, be supporting the King and helping him and his followers, and yet remain in complete ignorance of each other's efforts.

Chapter XIII

A Letter for Katharine

THE owls awoke Katharine, shrieking and screeching in the trees behind the mill as though partaking in some ghoulish battle. Unable to sleep, she knelt on the bed, under the window, and tried to see what was the cause of the disturbance. Now and again a shape glided past the panes and it seemed impossible to believe that such silent winged creatures could give vent to such frightening noises. It was dark outside; the landing-stage, the cobbles, the water and the trees mingled into one in the blackness of the night.

As she watched, Katharine's muscles stiffened and she turned her head into the room. Underneath, on the lower landing, someone was opening a door very slowly and making it creak with every inch it was pushed. It might be the miller, she thought, returning from Mudeford, but he had no need to be so cautious when everyone knew he was out. Curiosity overcoming her, she went to her own door and opened it with more success. A firm grip and a quick pull made a gap wide enough for her to slip through. A weird shadow hovered on the wall in the well of the stairs. It was Master Hogg, a naked candle in one hand, his boots in the other, arms outspread like an ungainly crow, trying to keep his balance on the tips of his stockinged feet. He passed the miller's room, which was apparently still unoccupied for the darkness yawned deeply into it, continued to the bottom of the stairs and into the living-room.

Katharine strained her ears to hear what he was doing, but the owls drowned such distant sounds. Suddenly, the owls were quiet, as though someone had put them in a box and closed the lid. She darted back to the bed and squeezed her head through the narrow window. Master Hogg had appeared on the cobbles and it was the sight of him that had silenced the owls. Katharine could imagine them, a truce declared, sitting in solemn rows on the branches overhead, regarding him with round, unblinking eyes and deciding that he was too large a beast to be tackled.

Master Hogg, with little concern for secrecy, stood his candle on the ground, where its flame wavered in the wind, while he tugged his boots up his legs. When they were on, he cupped his fingers round the light and spread them again three times. It was obviously a signal for someone hiding in the bushes across the road to approach. A tall, broad figure, a face which showed for an instant in the glow of the candle before it was extinguished, and Katharine immediately recognized Giles. She stared perplexed into the void below.

'Shall we talk here?' Giles's voice, though low, drifted up to the window.

'No, by the Priory.'

Footsteps kept deliberately soft crunched on the stones and faded out of earshot. An owl squeaked; Katharine slid back on to her heels more bewildered and puzzled than she had been on going to bed. The miller had a plan, Master Hogg had a plan. They could be separate plans, or one and the same, and for all she knew, Mistress Tuck might be out there in the dark, too.

'It would make it very much easier,' she thought, 'if I was told what they were all doing.' She waited hopefully for one of them to return, but the seconds dragged into long minutes and her head drooped on her arms.

In the morning when she realized that she had overslept, she dressed hurriedly, with a feeling of apprehension that something was about to go wrong. On reaching the living-room she saw that the two men had already eaten and had left the remains of their meal scattered over the table. There was a pan of cold, sticky porridge by the fire which was burning grey and dully. She piled on some turfs, poured some goat's milk from a jug into a bowl and cut herself some thick slices of bread and honey, which she ate standing at the open door.

The miller was working outside loading up a wagon with sacks of meal, his long shadow, thrown by the sunlight, running in bumps and curves across the uneven cobbles.

'Master Hogg is riding all day and will not be back until after dark,' he said, coming to speak to her. 'Mistress Tuck will fetch the week's washing and she can take you down with her to Mudeford. There is little to do here.' His shadow stopped at her feet and his blue eyes smiled into her face.

A cloud passed over the sun, a few yellow leaves rose in a tiny whirlwind and Katharine shivered. Master Hogg had said there would be a frost and she could feel the chill in the air. She went indoors and began clearing the table. The miller had made no reference to his work of the previous night, but perhaps Mistress Tuck, in the seclusion of her cottage, would say what plans had been made.

Katharine washed the dishes, a task she disliked because of the bubbles of grease floating on the surface of the water in the tub. Her hands still smelt even after she had rinsed and dried them, for the balls of soap at the mill were not scented like the ones Hester made at home. As she staggered to the door with the heavy tub to tip the dirty water into the river, Mistress Tuck's little boat was nosing alongside the jetty.

Together they tied the clothes to be washed in a sheet, and with the bundle under her arm Katharine stepped carefully into the rocking boat. With neat, easy strokes Mistress Tuck rowed out into the wider stream, and the clacking of the mill receded into the distance.

'There's no better sound on a hot summer's day,' the widow said. 'When work's finished and there's naught to do but shell the peas in the sun, and the water's lapping your feet and the swans are sleeping in the shallows, it will make your head nod quicker than anything. The winters can be bleak, though, lonely and bitter cold, when the ice comes up from the river and the wind sweeps across the marshes. But there's plenty of food in the river and plenty of fuel in the marsh. We've never starved nor gone in want of a fire as many have in other parts.' The oars dipped regularly, almost without a splash, as Mistress Tuck, glad to have someone to talk to, continued, 'I've known the mill for thirty years; I came to it as a bride of sixteen and many an hour I wasted watching the wheel turning and planning what I'd do when the children came along. But it wasn't the Lord's will, and there were never any babes to be sung to sleep by its clacking, and the mill became our child, then. Although I couldn't lift the sacks or do any of the heavy work, I knew every part and every sound—when the stone's running blunt or the water's low in the stream, and how to tell the feel of the flour by my thumb.' She smiled, guiding the boat round the curves of the rushes as they moved out farther into the harbour. 'Knowing so much about the workings was a help to him——' she nodded up the river. 'I taught him what he hasn't learnt from experience.'

'He told me how he came to be here,' Katharine murmured.

'Ay, we hid him up in your little room for nigh on four weeks, in the January it was, of '45. That's a year I'll not forget, with the town in such a state after the battle that Parliament had to send down timber to make good the damage. And before that, it was Waller's troopers all over the castle. Made out they took it without firing a shot, but that was a lie because I heard them. They had more than two hundred prisoners, though, because I saw the poor wretches lined up in the streets when they left for Andover.'

Katharine was no longer listening. At the mention of the year 1645, her thoughts had slipped away, for that year, the year of her father's disgrace and her brother's anger, was coloured like a bleak grey blot in her mind. As she looked at the red trunks of the pines at Mudeford, glowing like copper against the blue sky, as they drew nearer, that scene in the courtyard seemed more indistinct than it had ever been before. The words of the miller had partly been responsible for that, and the fact that she was not being constantly reminded of it by Hester. Hester, in her kindness and desire to try to make up for the experience and for what Katharine had lost, had made that day a ready excuse for childish lapses and frightened behaviour.

'We never thought we'd see him again, or that he would end up as the master of Place.' Mistress Tuck's voice broke through the memories as she guided the boat towards the shore. 'He wasn't meant to be a miller, he is too fond of his books, but there's plenty of time for thinking while you are waiting for the flour to run through the stones. Now, give me your hand, child, and mind your feet in the water.'

The nose of the boat scraped on the soft shingle and Mistress Tuck stepped over the prow on to the wet ground, and helped Katharine out after her. Katharine saw with interest, the fairylike island in the mist, the fishermen's cottages, some of them old and nearly falling down, and the swift, deep green channel. Mistress Tuck smiled as she noticed where her eyes had strayed.

'That is something men will never tame,' she remarked, pointing at the salmon run, which because the tide was low, was flowing smoothly out to sea unhindered and untouched by angry, white-capped waves. 'After a storm you never know where the salmon run will be in the morning and the harbour mouth may be fifty yards away with the sand all piled up in dunes where once was the sea. I would rather be up at the mill on a winter's night. Many a time down here I've thought the cottage would be swept away.'

She made the boat fast and led Katharine up the slope to her cottage, which had been one of a pair but its partner was now derelict. Behind it was a small garden surrounded by the pines, but with sufficient light and air to grow a few rows of vegetables. Mistress Tuck cut a cabbage and pulled some turnips. 'There,' she said, crumbling the soil from the white skins, ' they'll do to go in the remains of the stew from yesterday's supper and the cabbage can go on the boil as well.'

Indoors, Katharine found there was little time to be idle. A wooden tub was filled with hot water from the cauldron over the fire, soap was fetched and the dirty clothes were scrubbed and rubbed and twisted until Katharine thought they would be worn out. She was exhausted by the time they were rinsed and ready to be hung on the line in the wind. Her hands were sore, pink and wrinkled, her back ached and her cheeks were red with the exercise, so that she was not sorry when the bowls and spoons were laid out for their meal.

Afterwards, Mistress Tuck took her outside again, and up a flight of stone steps to the loft above the cottage.

'I think this is where the fishermen used to dry their nets,' she said, ' and it will do fine for your brother and his friends to hide in. They can have a lantern, for there are shutters over the windows; there's bedding and plenty of blankets I can bring up and it will be easy enough to get extra food. What I can't get, the miller can, and bring it down by boat. He hopes they will be out of the country by the end of the week, but he's not told me which boat or which tide. He has made his arrangements here but whether they have agreed to trust him I'm not sure. He said last night he would have to see them after all.'

'Would—would he have sent someone else to speak to them? ' Katharine asked, her heart pounding as she remembered the meeting of Giles and Master Hogg.

'He has not asked me to do it and he would never risk sending you, so he will have to go himself,' was the reply. 'The fewer in a secret the safer, he once said to me.'

Katharine was silent. She dared not relate what she had seen in case it was something the miller had deliberately withheld. 'When will they come? ' she asked.

'They can come tonight if need be, I'm ready and I know he is.'

She had to be satisfied with that answer and for the remainder of the day she was kept as busy as she had been in the morning. When the washing was nearly dry, it was brought indoors and pressed with the heavy irons heated over the fire, folded carefully and wrapped in an old shawl ready to be taken back up the river.

The sun had set by the time Mistress Tuck pushed off from the shingle bank and rowed the boat up to the mill. She held on to the wooden jetty while Katharine clambered ashore.

'Put them round the fire to air,' she said, 'and if the miller's not in, I shouldn't wait for him. I will be here again in the morning.'

Katharine stood and watched as the boat glided away, wondering if she would ever be able to handle oars so easily. Her own few accomplishments seemed of little use in her present situation. She crossed the landing-stage to the cobbles. The mill was silent and deserted, a white pennant of smoke floated from the chimney, the miller's flat-bottomed boat half laden with sacks rolled on the rising swell, which washed into the usually calm inlet. On the steps sat the green-eyed cat.

'Eyes the colour of ripe gooseberries,' Katharine murmured, thinking of the stunted bushes in the neglected garden, which was guarded by the shaggy goat. 'I suppose he milks it himself,' she went on, and was thankful that that was not one of the tasks Mistress Tuck had wanted her to learn.

In the living-room she found that the fire had recently been made up and the other two cats, the ginger and the tabby, were lying full length in front of the smouldering depths. She placed the bundle of washing on the floor and spread the clean linen on stools around the hearth. Then she began laying the table for the miller's evening meal. She went to the dresser for his plate and tankard.

On the dresser, propped against a jug, where she had not noticed it before, was a folded piece of paper with the word 'Kate' printed in capital letters across it. Katharine picked it up. It was sealed with candle grease pressed down by a grubby thumb. She suddenly felt frightened and turned it over and over in her hands before she had the courage to open it. She had thought it might be from the miller and her eyes sped at once to the signature at the foot. It was from Nicholas. Although she went back to the beginning and tried to read the writing slowly, all the time she was hastening to the end, her mind racing ahead with thoughts conjured up by his blunt sentences.

The letter was polite but cold, telling that he, Giles and Matthew hoped to be out of the country in the very near future, possibly that night. He apologized for the unpleasantness he had caused her, which had forced her to leave the farm; he hoped she would return to Gloucester with Hester when he had gone. Although she had informed the miller of their names and whereabouts she was to tell him no more—that could be left to their judgment. She was to destroy the letter as soon as she had read it.

The paper quivered between Katharine's fingers. She was appalled by the news, for it was an abrupt ending to her reunion with her brother. He was still angry, he still misunderstood what she had done and if he was leaving so quickly she would never be able to explain her actions, and he would always think badly of her.

She walked slowly to the fire and, kneeling between the cats, placed the paper on the turfs. The smoke stained it brown, the corners began to curl and a spark danced along the edges like a little man with a lantern running through a forest, now seen, now hidden, until tinder-dry it was swallowed in a burst of flame. She continued to gaze where it had been.

'Who is helping them?' she asked aloud. Was the letter a result of Master Hogg's meeting with Giles, or of Mistress Tuck's preparations, or both? It could hardly be the miller, or Nicholas would not have told her to remain quiet and destroy the letter. If the miller had seen Nicholas he would have told him why she ran away, but the miller did not want to see Nicholas or to give his name. Perhaps Nicholas was wiser than she in not trusting the unknown man.

As if her thoughts had come to life, the door opened and the miller came into the room.

'How long have you been sitting in the dark, Kate?' he asked, putting a taper in the fire and lighting the candles.

She did not reply but watched him as he moved to the table and began eating his supper.

'Mistress Mouse,' he said gravely, 'Master Hogg has chosen a most suitable name for such a quiet little thing, come here and sit with me.'

Katharine obeyed, pulling a stool to his side and propping her chin on her hands.

'After tonight you need have no more worries,' his voice was scarcely above a whisper. 'They will all be safe.'

'With Mistress Tuck?' she asked softly.

'Probably: I must go to the farm, although I had hoped they would have trusted me without.'

'But they will, when they know who you are?' She studied his face anxiously.

'Your brother may not.' His answer was serious, without the flicker of a smile, and Katharine was afraid to question him any more. 'Is Master Hogg out?' he asked abruptly, and when she nodded he looked puzzled. 'For a merchant interested in Christchurch he seems to spend most of his time well away from it. A carter this afternoon said he thought he saw him as far afield as Southampton. Go to bed, Kate, he'll not wake you when he comes in and you will not hear me leave. In the morning I shall have good news.'

Katharine lit her candle and went. The miller's conversation had eased her, but his ignorance of Master Hogg's affairs had added to the confusion. The only clear thought in her mind as she sat on the bed and peered into the night outside the window, was that if Nicholas was going down to Mudeford she wanted to go, too, and see him. She could not part with him again on a misunderstanding; he had already been absent six years and this time it might be for ever.

She put out the candle, and waited until her eyes grew

used to the darkness and she could see the pattern of the trees against the sky. If she went, she would have to go alone, very soon, along the road she had only seen once on Master Hogg's map, through the pine woods and into Mistress Tuck's cottage. In the morning they might have sailed and it would be too late.

Chapter XIV

The Run

KATHERINE did not undress. With her mind fully made up, she waited on the bed for the miller's departure. She heard the outer door close, but as his soft shoes made no sound on the cobbles it was not until there was the faint splash of an oar that she knew he was already in his boat. By the time he had rowed to the farm, she thought, had talked to Nicholas and had brought them down, she could be in Mudeford with Mistress Tuck. As there was still no sign of Master Hogg, she wrapped a shawl over her head and shoulders as the widow had often done, tucking the ends through the lacing of her bodice, and crept down the stairs, through the living-room and on to the steps.

She paused for a moment, her back pressed against the wall, looking into the patchwork depths of the night. As always, the cats were in the mill, and one of them, no more than a tabby shadow, his curiosity too much for him, came to see what she was doing. His tail curved like a question mark against Katharine's skirt. She stooped and rubbed the vibrating body and then, neither running nor walking, but with a queer kind of breathless shuffle, she started up the path by the mill-stream. The whole world was in darkness; not a light showed anywhere as she reached the bridge in the town, and there was no sound except the lap of the river. She paused again on the bridge. It was the only exposed part of the road, for where it continued on the other side of the water it was shrouded in trees. Clutching her dress in her hands she ran across, hardly daring to breathe for fear someone would hear her, and stifled the painful gasps in the folds of her shawl before going on. The road was long and winding. Her eyes darted frequently to the shapeless bushes as she passed in case figures were lurking there to pounce; the trees almost met over her head, leaving a jagged line of clouded sky as faint as the dusty path under her feet.

From Master Hogg's map, Katharine could remember that the road went beyond Mudeford to a place called Lymington, and somewhere on the road was a little track to the right which went straight to the sea, circling the woods and down to the fishing hamlet. Although she had to go more slowly as the distance increased, she kept up a short, stiff pace which made her muscles ache; her chest ached because of her quick breathing and her throat ached because of her dry, parted lips.

She seemed to have gone so far and to have taken so long that she was beginning to think that she must soon see the houses on the outskirts of Lymington, when there was a gap in the trees and the sound of waves breaking on the shore. She slackened her speed with relief. Beyond the pines was Mistress Tuck's cottage and safety. The new lane ran by open ground, on one side of which was the sea, and she realized that she would be silhouetted against the light water if there was anyone, a poacher, a fisherman or just a night prowler abroad at that hour. If she cut through the copse, she thought, she would be hidden and could slip into the cottage garden over the hedge at the back.

She turned in cautiously among the trees. The ground was soft with fallen needles, and where the pines had thinned, bushes and tangled undergrowth had taken their place. Katharine pushed the branches aside, but the noise of the crackling twigs was drowned by the wind above and the sea rolling on the beach. Tense again with the effort of finding a way to the cottage, her eyes straining as far as they could see and her ears accustomed to the rhythm of the water, a different sound, a quick frightened movement as quick as her own, was enough to hold her poised and motionless, listening, watching, biting her lips to prevent herself from crying out.

A great dark shape was snuffling towards her, head down,

neck stretched, and a nose rubbed into her cheek and shawl. It was a horse. Katharine's fingers, outspread at first to protect herself, felt the warmth of its skin as she gently caressed it, sliding her hands up to the ears and mane. She discovered at once that it was not a horse left out to graze, for she touched bit, bridle and saddle in quick succession. Immediately she thought of Master Hogg and his meeting with Giles, and the letter from Nicholas. The horse whinnied softly as if glad to have company in the dark wood.

'Can't you keep those animals still up there,' came a hushed, irritated voice from the road.

Katharine prickled all over with the sudden rush of blood, which receded again leaving her cold and trembling. Obviously there was more than one horse and more than one man concealed in the woods with her. A tongue clacked encouragingly and Katharine, unable to run away, slid to the ground where she was, like a ball of grey worsted in the swathed shawl. She hid her face and closed her eyes. Careful footsteps pushed through the undergrowth, a boot brushed her skirt and she sensed the arm over her head as the horse was caught and turned.

'Come on, lad,' murmured a voice. 'Quietly now.'

The animal was led away nearer the road and on opening her eyes, Katharine watched until she could see and hear it no more. She wriggled to her feet and with added caution, for fear there were others straying among the trees, she crept towards the cottages. She reached the hedge bordering Mistress Tuck's garden and crouched in its shelter, peering between the thin stems at the dark patch of vegetables. There was not a glimmer of light and all sounds were swallowed up by the roaring of the run below the shingle bank.

Not daring to stand upright, Katharine squirmed through the hedge and crawled awkwardly on hands and knees to the steps leading to the loft where she had been in the afternoon. It would be easier, she thought, to climb up there first and see if Giles and Nicholas were there or if the room had been prepared in expectation of them, for Mistress Tuck might even be there herself.

At the top of the steps the door was on a hook, which Katharine lifted so that the thick wood swung inwards on well-oiled hinges. The door swung into darkness and a deserted room, as bare as when she had seen it hours before. The shutters were fastened back from the glassless windows, and the noise of the sea and wind poured into the emptiness, filling it with an uncanny roar of desolation. Katharine stood on the threshold in dismay. She had been so sure she would find them — the miller had suggested the possibility, he had said he would have good news for her in the morning, Nicholas had written to say he was leaving, and there were the horses in the wood.

'Master Hogg must be helping them,' she murmured. 'He must be helping them tonight and the miller does not know. By the time he reaches the farm they will have gone, and I shall never see Nicholas again.'

All her courage and strength ebbed from her and she sank into a limp heap on the floor, knowing that she could not face the road back to the mill and the horsemen hiding in the copse. She would go down to Mistress Tuck, tell her everything that had happened — she was tired of secrets — and ask if she could stay the remainder of the night. After that, she would go to the farm, and be restored to Hester and the house in Gloucester as her brother wished. Katharine shivered, for the memory of the broken house only made her more miserable, and the dank, neglected garden there was guarded by a ghost more real and more frightening than the miller's goat behind his gooseberry bushes.

She stood up and closed the door, hooking it securely. Steadying herself against the stones she started to go down on the side leading to the cottage entrance. Her foot scraped on the surface, she swayed, balanced in mid-air, unable to move, for beneath her, his body outlined on the white wall, head turned in the direction of the harbour, a man was sitting.

Silently, Katharine withdrew her foot, sliding it backwards until it touched the door and she was able to grip the solid wood.

'Here,' the man's head jerked sharply at the sound of the low whisper and another figure joined him on the steps. 'They've no hope once they've landed.' His voice, raised to be heard above the water, carried up to Katharine. 'The beach is guarded—I've men in the wood, each side of the road and the marsh——'

'They should be on the headland by now, with the bridge closed behind them,' the other interrupted. 'There will be a lantern flashed from the boat while they are being rowed across the harbour—that is your signal to be ready. The boy is down there with the lantern to show them where to land.'

For a moment the voices were lost as the heads were bent together. Katharine's fingers grew numb while she listened. Who were they talking about? Who were they waiting for with guarded beach and hidden horsemen? Who would have no hope once they had landed?

'They think there's a long boat ready to take them out to a vessel off the Island—it won't sail for France, though——' There was a stifled laugh. 'He'll not slip through the net as he did at Charmouth.'

Katharine started as she caught the last word, the name of the little village which had twice been mentioned in connection with the King. She shifted her foot to ease her weight. On the back of Master Hogg's map had been the queried months, September and October; the miller had answered her abruptly when she had asked if the King could possibly come to Christchurch to escape to France. Could the miller and Master Hogg be down there in the gloom by the harbour making a plot to trap the King? Or were they helping him to escape, believing that there was a boat as arranged, only to fall into this neatly laid snare?

'I will go back to the boy. Another ten to fifteen minutes and we should see the signal.'

One man stood up and moved out of sight, while the other rested his head on the wall, whistling very softly through his teeth until, realizing the risk he was running, he stopped and continued to tap his knees in time with the silent tune.

Katharine, stiff with cold now that she had cooled after the long walk, stared down at him. 'What am I to do?' she thought. 'If only I could wake Mistress Tuck, and where, where are Nicholas and Giles?' For all she knew they might be there with the King, in the escape that would lead to disaster unless she did something to prevent it. She could not reach Mistress Tuck with a man sitting on the doorstep, and a woman and child would be of little use against the army which seemed to be hidden around the cottage. For once, she would have to act alone with no one to guide her; the other alternative would be to remain in the loft and watch the boats rowing towards the flashing lantern and the inevitable result. The boy with the lantern was her only chance. If she could stop him from answering the signal from the boat, the rowers might, seeing no sign of where to land, suspect that something was wrong and alter their course. Already, unerringly and in ignorance, she had walked through the unseen circle of soldiers in the pine copse, but it was almost too much to hope that she would be able to do it again, down to the boy on the beach.

She was surprised at her own calmness. Always before, when dangers, however slight, had threatened her she had been terrified; now, she seemed to have forgotten herself and was only thinking of the fate awaiting the fugitives in the boat.

She tugged the shawl tightly over her head and shoulders again, for its warmth and closeness gave her confidence, and, moving stealthily from the door of the loft, crept down the way she had come into Mistress Tuck's garden. She groped along the back wall of the cottage, expecting all the time that instead of stones her fingers would touch the roughness of a man's clothing. No one was there and she safely passed

the end of the ruined building, squeezed through the hedge and stood hesitating on the edge of the thinning pine copse.

The trunks of the trees were slim and gaunt, hardly seen against the black water behind them; only the roar and occasional spume of white spray thrown in the air showed that the sea was pounding below. By one fearful step at a time, her dress twisted firmly in her hands so that it would not catch on loose twigs, Katharine crossed the copse to the beach. The tide was nearly in, heaving the waves into the gullies of the rocks, sucking and gurgling at the shingle as it slithered out again. If there were men hiding among the boulders Katharine saw none, and no one could have seen her, as inch by inch, she crawled and clambered nearer to the fishermen's little wooden jetty. It was there, she thought, that the boy must be with the lantern, for it was almost opposite the widow's cottage.

Her outstretched hands, feeling for the next firm foothold, came in contact with a rope which swayed and slackened as the water rose and fell. It was evidently that of a boat tied up for the night; beyond it was another, the prow of the boat drawn up on the beach. She knelt behind it and peered over the top. Within a few feet of her, also kneeling on the wet ground, were two dim shapes with a shuttered lantern between them, for a crack of light leaked from a slit in the cover and trickled over the pebbles. Katharine sank back and lay still on her side. She had succeeded in finding the boy with the lantern, but there was a man with him and she did not know how to stop the signal.

She stared across the water to the low sandbanks on the other shore. It was impossible to see where water and sand met; but the sky, being a lighter shade than anything else, showed the faint outline of the dunes under the headland. Suddenly, there was a pinprick of light in the blackness; it winked unsteadily, hovering like a will-o'-the-wisp on the surface of the sea. Katharine sat up — it was the boat carrying the fugitives, the King was coming and she had done nothing to stop him. She looked at the two on the other side of her boat. They were as alert as she was, the lantern already moved to a better position. Katharine's mind worked wildly. There were two of them, not just one boy. Should she run up, snatch the lantern and throw it away? Should she shout at them not to wave it? While she was thinking, the lantern was held up, unshuttered and tossed violently to and fro, its beam flaming over the beach and the short, stocky man, who swung the boy's arm backwards and forwards.

Katharine sprang to her feet, caution and her own safety forgotten. She darted back across the beach to the boat floating in deep water under the rocks; feverishly, she tugged at the painter holding it to the shore, and glanced again over the harbour mouth.

'Go back, go back,' she screamed at the bobbing light which, like the single eye of an enormous dragon, was moving slowly nearer. 'They will kill you — there are soldiers.'

As she loosened the rope and pushed the boat as she had seen Mistress Tuck do, there was a shout behind her. She flung herself in afterwards, the little craft rocked, nearly capsizing with her awkwardness, she lost her balance and lay stunned and shaken on the bottom boards, feebly groping for oars or paddles. She could feel none and knew that if there had been any she would not have been able to use them. Her weight and the sudden jerk had sent the boat spinning beyond the shelter of the jetty, where the larger waves seized it, and tossed it upon their white caps and rolled it down their smooth black sides.

Katharine slid to her knees, coughing and choking as the water poured in, soaking her to the skin. Bearing down upon her was the yellow eye, still creeping inexorably towards the shore.

'Don't land,' she cried again, and her voice sounded thin and shrill. 'There are soldiers waiting.'

For an instant the eye rose above her, a huge wave smacked the boat, there was the grinding and smashing of woodwork, yells, shouts, and then water, nothing but ice-cold water sweeping over her head. Katharine struggled and gasped. 'Master Hogg—it was Master Hogg,' she tried to say, but the sea swallowed and silenced the puny cry, ringing and seething in her ears as she sank below the surface.

Chapter XV

A Puddle of Water

KATHARINE'S flailing arms touched something solid, which she clutched at frantically. A voice swore at her. 'Stop struggling, child, or you'll drown us both. Take your arms from my neck and keep still.'

It was impossible for her to obey. Afraid that if she loosened her grip, she would disappear again beneath the black water, she struggled and fought until a sharp blow nearly knocked her unconscious. 'Heaven help me if I've hurt her,' went on the voice. An arm was slipped under her unresisting shoulders, her head raised above the waves, and very slowly she felt she was being dragged towards the shore.

'Try to hold on to this,' the voice said.

Katharine's weak fingers felt the branch of a tree which had been worn smooth by the tides. It was firm, buried deeply in the shingle, but her frenzied strength of a few moments ago had gone.

'I can't,' she choked, gasping for breath and coughing up quantities of salt water.

She was lifted until her body was wedged in a fork, where she hung limply like a piece of seaweed, swaying with the movement of the waves. A hand still gripped her waist and the voice continued to speak.

'Try to hold, Kate, just a little. I must help Nicholas.'

She realized then that it was Giles talking to her and was too stupefied to wonder how he had been able to come to her aid so quickly. He went on supporting her, his muscles straining against the pull of the current, his eyes staring into the darkness for a sight of his friend, whose head might be visible on the heavy swell. Behind their shelter there was a flash of light and dull reports as shots were fired into the channel.

'They've seen us,' Giles muttered, 'but if they fire like that they will kill their own men.'

As if in answer to his thoughts, the firing ceased. The soldiers, who had been hidden in the trees and on the beach, made no secret of their presence. Amid shouts and half-heard commands they lit lanterns and launched a boat from the little jetty, while the inhabitants of the few cottages, awakened by the commotion, flung open their shuttered windows and demanded to know what was happening.

There were several heads showing in the water, but the tiny beam from the light only lit the faces of those manning the boat and scarcely made any impression on the dark expanse of waves. As the boat swung into the open, Giles saw two figures turn in its direction and swim towards it.

'Their men,' he murmured, but there were still two more heads where there should only have been one, and that the one belonging to Nicholas. He watched anxiously. A soldier from the shore must have jumped in with the intention of capturing a fugitive even if he risked drowning himself by doing so. As Nicholas was not a strong swimmer, he would need every effort to keep his head above water, without having to use his energy for defending himself as well. Giles released Katharine, who slipped a few inches out of the tree. He pulled at her sodden shawl, which was still wrapping her shoulders, tied one end round her waist and wound the rest over the branch.

'Hold on,' he commanded, hoping that in her present weak state an instinctive desire to live would keep her clinging to the support. Then he struck out powerfully to the two men, who were only a few yards distant.

'Nick!' he shouted. 'Nick!' He was giving away their whereabouts, but there was only the other swimmer who would realize it and he could be quickly dealt with.

Instead of the cry encouraging Nicholas, his strokes seemed

feebler and for, a moment, he was buried in the trough of a breaker. When he reappeared Giles saw that he was being held up by the second man. He approached, ready to snatch an unconscious Nicholas from the arms of his captor.

'A ball grazed his head—he's not badly hurt—stunned for a minute,' the supposed soldier gasped. 'Is Katharine safe? I heard her cry out.'

It was not the time to ask for explanations, and Giles, with a quick word that Katharine was unharmed, guided them both under the protection of the tree. As soon as Nicholas felt something firm, he seemed to recover, and tried to wipe the blood from his face with his streaming sleeve. Giles hooked Katharine in the curve of his arm again; she was numb with cold and only the shawl had prevented her from being washed away. As the boat drew in to the jetty there was another burst of firing.

'It is no use trying to land,' Nicholas's rescuer whispered. 'We shall have to swim for it, up the river, and I will hide you in the mill. If they don't find you on the marsh they may think you have drowned. Give the child to me—you watch her brother, he may not last the distance. Keep as close to me as you can, the harbour is treacherous.'

Giles guessed immediately that it was the miller of Place, for there was no one else who could be so familiar with their names and relationship. He swung Katharine into the man's arms.

'Now, Mistress Mouse,' said the miller, as he gripped her shoulders; and the odd name in those frightening circumstances had a ring of safety about it. 'You have already saved our lives once, but this is going to be far worse than any drowning in the salmon run. Keep still, for if you struggle, not one of us will have the strength to quieten you and we shall all be captured.'

He was right. It was far worse than anything Katharine had experienced before. She was on her back, fighting the terrible desire to wriggle over and grapple with her supporter as she had done with Giles. Water washed into her eyes and ears, and she was stiff with cold and fear, thereby making the miller's task all the more difficult. Her only comfort was that Giles was swimming at her side, his head turned towards Nicholas, ready to help him if he showed signs of flagging.

Eventually, under the posts of his own little landing-stage, the miller groped and clung to the wood. Giles and Nicholas joined him and the three hung there, too exhausted to speak. Giles recovered first. He clambered up on to the platform.

'Let me have Katharine,' he said. He pulled her up and let her fall limply at his feet. Nicholas followed and crouched by his sister.

'Where is Matthew?' the miller asked, still in the water.

'He was with Master Hogg on the beach,' Giles replied; concern for his brother had been nagging at him all through the swim up the river.

'Master Hogg? What——? Never mind, there is no time now.' The miller's hands slipped from the landing-stage. 'Find yourselves some dry clothes—there are plenty in the linen chest. If Master Hogg comes home before I do, don't open the door to him; he may be your friend but there is no need to let him know you are hiding in my mill. I am going back for your brother.' Ignoring the murmur of protest, the miller struck out smoothly and noiselessly into the darkness.

Giles turned to Nicholas, who had raised Katharine on to his shoulder and was walking towards the mill. Leaving a trail of water behind, they crossed the cobbles, went up the steps and into the living-room. A rush of warm air from the smouldering fire greeted them as they entered. The door was bolted, the fire beaten into life with a generous supply of logs, not the usual turfs which burned slowly, and the candles lit.

Giles dripped around the room. 'The linen chest must be upstairs, I can't see it here,' he muttered. 'Get Katharine dry and I will bring blankets down with me.' He took off his own shirt and hose and wrung them into the bucket near the door, before padding away in his bare feet.

Nicholas propped his sister against the beam of the hearth and began tugging at the soaked strings of her bodice.

'You will knot them,' she protested feebly, between chattering teeth.

His answer to that was a flick from the knife at his belt, and he peeled the sodden layers from her like the skin from an onion. She was rubbed dry with the neatly folded linen which had been left round the fire to air, and rolled tightly in the old shawl.

'Why don't you dry yourself?' she whispered, gasping for breath under the vigorous treatment.

When Giles re-entered the room with his arms full of an assortment of clothes, and a blanket, which he wrapped around Katharine, Nicholas did as he was asked. Between them they had breeches, stockings, shirts and jackets. They turned out the dresser for a flask of spirits, which they drank neat and forced Katharine, much against her wishes, to swallow diluted in hot water. They extinguished the candles so that if Master Hogg came back he would not see the light through the door, shuttered the window and sat on the hearth in the glow of the fire.

'Now, Kate,' Nicholas began. 'What were you doing down by the harbour at that time of night?'

Katharine felt secure and warm. Wrapped in the grey blanket, with her hair streaking over her face, she looked like some sea creature emerging from its shell.

'I had your letter,' she stammered awkwardly. 'You were angry and I wanted to tell you why I ran away—I did not think I should ever see you again and I wanted to say good-bye.'

'How did you know we would be at Mudeford at that hour?'

'Because I thought the miller was helping you and he had gone to the farm—but—but the King——' She tried to wriggle to her feet at the recollection of the conversation on the steps. 'They said the King was there—in the boat coming across from the headland—Master Hogg was there on the beach with a boy who was to wave a lantern; that was the signal for the soldiers to be ready.'

Giles and Nicholas looked at each other in mystification. 'There was no one with us, Kate,' Giles explained. 'The boy was Matthew, he was with Master Hogg. That was all arranged to guide us—we came over the bridge to——'

'And they closed the bridge behind you so that you could not escape,' Katharine interrupted. 'The beach and the woods were surrounded and the boat was going to take you to another, off the Island, which would not sail for France. I heard it all. Why did you ever trust Master Hogg? He had a map, I saw it, with all the tides and shipping marked, and about the King last being seen at Charmouth. Why did you trust him? The miller would not, although he did not know anything about him.'

'We had no reason to trust the miller either,' Giles said gently.

'But you had,' Katharine retorted. 'He sent Mistress Tuck to you, but Nicholas chose to think ill of me and thought the man to whom I had confided most about you was less reliable than a complete stranger.'

Nicholas, silenced by his sister's torrent of words, took the rebuke humbly, and they both let her continue her story without further interruptions. She told them about Mistress Barfutt, who, now that they had left the farm would be more suspicious of Hester, about the miller and about seeing the meeting from the window. Giles realized again that his resemblance to the King had caused the trouble. Master Hogg had fallen easily for their plan once they had met in the Priory grounds, almost too easily it seemed now, for he had made his arrangements for their escape with alarming speed. The net had been flung wide and would be wider still, with the whole countryside swarming with soldiers, if they thought the King was hiding in the area. Giles looked grave, for their position was serious. They were in the centre of the marsh, which would be thoroughly searched; Matthew was missing, the miller was missing, and at any moment the man whom they had trusted — and it was only Katharine's brief glimpse in the dark which had cast suspicion upon him — might return to the mill and find them. The one gleam of light in the black situation was that by their misfortune they might have distracted attention from the real quarry, the King, and made it easier for him to pass by unnoticed.

'Katharine must go to bed,' Giles said, 'and this room be cleared so that nothing remains to arouse doubt in anyone's mind.'

Nicholas picked up his sister, and she was given a candle, which she shone to guide him up the stairs to her room. Giles stayed below. With little respect for Mistress Tuck's freshly laundered sheets, he mopped the floor, wrung out their clothes and piled them in the hearth, to be removed quickly if there were footsteps outside.

After a time he heard the latch rattle and a soft voice calling their names. Prepared for trouble, he went to the door and opened it. The miller entered alone, shot the bolt behind him and puddled across the floor to the settle. He sat down heavily, and in the firelight he looked exhausted. Giles handed him the flask of spirits.

'You have not swum both ways again?' he asked, almost reproachfully.

The miller shook his head slowly. 'Only across. I could not find the boy. There were soldiers on the road to Mudeford, but they had no prisoners. He may be with Master Hogg or he may have gone back to the farm — I will find out in the morning.' He smoothed back his wet hair and shook the drips from his hand into the fire, which hissed angrily. 'Where is Nicholas?' he asked.

'Up with Katharine, putting her to bed,' Giles replied. 'She has surprised him tonight. He did not think she had so much courage.'

'She has plenty of courage, but she is afraid of herself,' the miller answered. He was gazing into the bright flames on the logs, making no attempt to dry himself. He appeared to have forgotten that he was so wet, although the pool of water at his feet was growing gradually larger. 'I went to Virgin to-night,' he went on quietly, 'in an effort to make you trust me, because I had failed previously.' He smiled, but did not look at Giles, who began to feel uncomfortable. 'It was fortunate that I did, because when I returned to the mill and found Katharine gone, I thought she could only be with Mistress Tuck, and I was in my boat there, by the run, when it all happened. If I had found you, I was prepared to tell you my name, because that would have been proof enough of my intentions; but I also wrote a letter, which I would have given to Matthew if I was unsuccessful. As you know, I did not find you, for you were away on your own route of escape and—' he paused—'I was unwise enough to leave the message on a pallet in your loft. I am sorry, I had no idea where you were, I hoped you would be back, but it is there for anyone to see, and a few hours is the longest you dare stay here.'

'But you—' Giles exclaimed in horror at the man's lack of concern for himself—'you will never be safe at the mill again and——' And it was all their fault, he was going to say. If Nicholas had believed his sister and gone to see her as Giles had wanted, the letter would never have been written.

'If I can reach the farm in the morning to look for Matthew there is a chance of retrieving the letter as well,' the miller went on, with hollow reassurance.

At that moment Nicholas entered the room. He went straight to the dripping figure on the settle, clasped his hands gratefully and thanked him for helping Katharine and for saving him at the harbour mouth. He was unaware of the miller's slight hesitation and his reluctance to stand in the full light of the fire. Giles, more observant, noticed and wondered.

Without further conversation the miller led them in the dark through the empty mill, up the stairs past the crouching

cats, who hid in the corners, large-eyed and alert with curiosity at the invasion of their nightly property, and into the granary at the top. There, behind the bins and hutches, he gave them sacking for bedding and warned them to be ready at daybreak to follow his instructions.

He returned to the living-room, rearranged the steaming clothes around the hearth, glanced at the bolted door and went upstairs. He undressed, put on his long nightshirt and loose gown and crept down to the fire again, where, listening for sounds on the cobbles, he tried to dry his own and Katharine's garments as quickly as possible. If neither of them had anything to wear in the morning, it would need more ingenuity than he possessed to deceive Master Hogg. When almost satisfied, he folded them, tucked them under one arm and the damp bundle belonging to Giles and Nicholas under the other, covered the fire, unlatched the door and went to bed.

Ten minutes later Master Hogg rode down the lane by the mill-stream. He stabled his horse and, with his usual consideration for the sleepers in the mill, removed his boots on the doorstep before entering. He let out a stifled ejaculation of discomfort as his stockinged foot descended into a puddle of cold water. With extreme caution, he picked up his boots, unfastened the door, bolted it again and stood quite still in the closely shuttered room, with his round head raised and his nose sniffing the air like a dog's at the hunt.

'Spirits,' he muttered.

He tiptoed across the floor in the direction of the fire, moving slowly because of the darkness, until his gloved fingers groped for the cover, which he lifted.

'A-ah,' he breathed softly, on seeing the height and quantity of the glowing embers. He replaced the cover and stood up, taking off his hat and stuffing his gloves inside with a thoughtful, serious expression on his face which was unusual.

Down on the shingle, some time earlier, before the riot of shots and shouts, he had heard a voice, a girl's voice, crying over the water for a boat not to land, and it had been a voice remarkably like that of the miller's niece. He had been ready to scoff at himself for having such a fantastic idea—until he had stepped in the puddle at the door. There had been no rain all day—someone might have upset a bucket; but the banked fire, the heavy, lingering smell, both pointed to another, more interesting reason, for his soaked stockings.

Chapter XVI

Mistress Barfutt's Triumph

A COMPLETELY bewildered Matthew, who had lost all his former confidence, was making his way across the deserted yard of Virgin Farm. He had no idea what had happened to his brother and Nicholas. Earlier that night he had followed the instructions Master Hogg had given him. He had met the merchant at the town bridge and together they had gone on foot to Mudeford. There, hidden from the cottages, they had waited on the narrow strip of shingle, and although Matthew's eyes had soon become accustomed to the darkness, down by the water's edge the night seemed overpowering. He wanted to shout at the waves to stop roaring, the pines to stop swaying, the clouds to break, if only for a moment, in order to let him listen for other sounds and see more than the heaving water and black rim of the marsh.

Master Hogg, who had handed him the lantern telling him to flash it when the light from the boat crossing the channel was shown, had disappeared frequently—to see if the other boat was secure farther round on the beach, he said every time he returned. To Matthew's tired eyes, after a while, the whole surface of the water had seemed alive with imaginary boats, and when the signal came he was not prepared, and Master Hogg had impatiently jerked him to his feet, shaken the cover from the lantern and waved Matthew's arm on high. Then, had come confusion. First, a boy's cry calling for the boat not to land, an exclamation of anger from Master Hogg, shouts from unseen men, and then Matthew had ducked as shots spattered from behind.

'An ambush, get back to the farm,' Master Hogg had hissed in his ear. 'I will reach the others.' Matthew had obeyed, too frightened by the sudden disaster to do anything else, and hoping that if he took care of himself there would be more chance of help for his brother. He had not wanted to be separated from Giles and Nicholas, but in order not to let Master Hogg know they were connected with each other, those two had had to pretend they were coming over the heath from the direction of Poole, across the bridge over the Stour and on to the headland. Once they had been rowed out to the vessel off the Island, Matthew was to be smuggled aboard. Now, it was all over.

Matthew groped to the door of the barn, which he had thought he was never going to see again, climbed the ladder and stood miserably in the empty loft, wondering what he ought to do. He was uneasy because of Master Hogg's reactions to the ambush. The man had been angry, not alarmed, at the unexpected development—angry with Matthew for being slow, angry at the unknown voice shouting at the boat. Why should anyone want to shout at a boat carrying Giles and Nicholas, Matthew asked himself. Why should two men who had taken part in a fatal duel, for that was their final story which they had told Master Hogg, have a party of soldiers waiting for them on the shore? And what had happened to them now? They might be drowned, or with Master Hogg, or captured, or trying to get back to the farm. If they were not back at the farm by the morning he would have to invent some excuse for their absence to give to Mistress Barfutt, and at the first opportunity, return himself to the beach at Mudeford. He sat down on his bed thoughtfully, and slowly pulled off his shoes and coat. As there was nothing he could do until daylight, he supposed he ought to try to get some rest. He hooked his coat on the wood above his brother's pallet, rolled on his blanket, and closed his eyes in fitful sleep.

In the morning, the deserted pallets on either side were an unpleasant reminder of what had happened. Matthew, disconsolate in the cold, grey light, ran his fingers through his hair and put on his coat. As he tugged it from the beam where he had hung it the night before, a piece of paper fell to the ground. Curiously turning it over, he saw that it was a letter addressed to Nicholas. Without a qualm of conscience, for if Nicholas were not there it seemed only sensible that someone should know what it contained, he broke the seal and read the sheet. Although the handwriting was black and not easy to decipher he soon realized that it was a message from the miller of Place, offering help for their escape. The writer ended by saying that as proof of his fidelity he gave his true name, which Nicholas could not fail to remember. Matthew shrugged his shoulders, for he was not familiar with it, but Giles, who was older, might certainly have heard it. The final request was that the letter should be destroyed.

Matthew, with the folded sheet in his hand, looked round the loft. The tinder-box and lantern had gone, he had had them on the beach with him at Mudeford, and the only other sure way of destruction was by the fire in the farm kitchen when he went for his breakfast. He twisted the letter into a spill, brushed the dust from his jacket, put on his shoes and went down the ladder into the barn. If Giles and Nicholas did not return, he thought, he would not trouble about Master Hogg but go down to the mill and ask the miller for his aid and advice. With more confidence and assurance than he had felt for some hours, he walked out across the yard, stopping at the pump to rinse his face and hands in the ice-cold water which spurted out as he swung the handle.

In the kitchen, the trestles were up and laden with food placed there by Mistress Barfutt. She fed her labourers well, giving them two large meals a day. 'You'll get no work out of a hungry maid or man,' she had once said to Hester, who had expressed surprise at the pies, tarts, beef, mutton, quantities of rich milk, butter, ale, new bread and honey spread before the farm hands. That was the one aspect of life at Virgin Farm that Matthew enjoyed.

He edged into his place beside Barney the carter, who

had his plate piled high and was burying his face in a full tankard.

'Where's the others?' the man asked, for ever since their arrival with Mistress Hester the three servants had always been together. 'Like three folks from foreign parts,' Barney had confided to the ploughman. 'And what with their strange talk from up north, they're about as hard to understand.'

'Sick,' Matthew mumbled, stuffing his mouth with food so that he would not be able to speak.

Barney's eyes grew round over the top of his tankard, his cheeks swelled with the inrush of ale which he was unable to swallow because of the rumble of laughter bursting up his windpipe.

'Sick!' he exploded, and Matthew turned his cheek away to wipe it with his sleeve. 'Sick! Drunk, drunk as lords, I'll be bound.' He waggled a finger at Matthew's astounded face. 'I saw them,' he said. 'I saw them, creeping off for a carousal in the town.'

Matthew's colour flamed at the unexpected revelation.

'There is no need to tell Mistress Barfutt,' he muttered, 'They—they may have recovered later.'

'She won't need no telling, she's got a nose like a ferret for smelling out idlers. She'll have them out in the yard with their heads under the pump before you nor I could stop her.' Barney gave him a meaning look which Matthew could not interpret and took a large bite of pie which he chewed rabbit-like on his few sound teeth. 'She's not about yet,' he murmured.

Matthew glanced round the room and realized by the babel of noise that Sarah Barfutt was not busy by the ovens as she had been on every other morning. His fingers crumpled the twist of paper in his pocket. If he could get near enough, it was an opportunity to toss the letter into the fire, but any action of his at the moment would be regarded with suspicion by the sharp-eyed carter. Suddenly, the chatter in the kitchen ceased; all eyes were turned to the door, where Mistress Barfutt had appeared. Behind her, the daylight was blocked by tall, helmeted figures. A girl screamed.

'Lord save us, there's soldiers come to the farm!'

'Be quiet!' her mistress commanded, her black eyes scanning the tables. 'I sent for them. Where are the servants of my Cousin Hester?'

Matthew gripped the bench on which he was sitting and did not move. Barney nudged him. 'Go on,' he said. 'You're one.'

Matthew stood up, very slowly. 'Here, ma'am,' he whispered hoarsely.

She glared at him. 'And the others?' she snapped.

He hesitated. 'Not here, yet.'

'Fetch them,' she ordered.

Matthew sprang forward ready to obey, for if he could get through that phalanx of Cromwellian uniform he would not stop running until he reached the mill. Mistress Barfutt was not so easily tricked. She stopped him with a wave of the arm, and sent one of the hands sitting nearer the door to go on the errand. As the soldiers parted to let the man go past, Matthew, acting on the impulse of the moment, darted to the fire. There was a roar and a mighty rush into the room, stools were flung over, the dairy-maids shrieked, Barney leapt to save his toppling platter, and Matthew was tripped with a well-placed boot and went headlong into the hearth, sending fire-irons and pans of scalding water spinning on to the floor. Heedless of the pain, he thrust his whole hand and the deadly letter into the flames of the fire; gloved fingers twisted his wrist, wrenching the paper from his grasp as he was tossed face downwards, and a heavy foot was pushed violently into his back.

He lay still, eyes closed, body limp with hopelessness, dimly hearing the sounds as the room was quietly and hurriedly set in order by the frightened girls.

'Where are they? Have they gone?' It was Mistress Barfutt's voice raised in anger and disappointment. 'The boy will know, I thought he was lying.'

'I saw them.' That was Barney's gleeful interruption. 'I saw them creeping off last night for a carousal in the town. They're dead drunk by now or sleeping it off by the roadside.'

Mistress Barfutt silenced him. 'Enough, man, you know nothing of them. They are Royalist fugitives and one of them was the King.'

A murmur of fear and wonder greeted her disclosure. Matthew felt her skirt brush his outstretched hand as she moved to the soldier who had pinned him to the ground.

'I suspected them from the first,' she began. 'These three fellows came from Gloucester with my Cousin Hester and a child they pretended was ill. No sooner were they here than up comes a Master Hogg—he is at the bottom of the whole scheme, he comes from Place Mill below the Priory, and the miller is in it too, he is not what he makes out to be—and Master Hogg asks for the boy to help him. He recognizes the servant Giles, the tall one I suspected was the King. I sent up to Ringwood, not a moment too soon as it turns out, for you to come down here. Now it looks as though they've slipped through our fingers and only the boy will be able to tell how.'

The boot was removed from Matthew's back and he was jerked to his feet. A titter of laughter ran through the room as he reappeared, for his clothes were stained and dappled with the upset contents of the stew pan. His arms were pinioned behind him and he was turned to face the officer who had tripped him, and in whose hands was the miller's crumpled letter, which had obviously been smoothed and read.

'Where are your cousin and this child?' the officer asked Mistress Barfutt.

He listened impatiently to her explanation that Katharine had run away to the mill, an explanation that only deepened the conspiracy when, on Hester being brought into the kitchen, he examined her pass and saw that she was a Roman Catholic. He ordered her immediate arrest.

'They must both be lodged in the castle at Christchurch, I can spare no men to return to Ringwood,' he said, indicating the two prisoners — Hester, weeping and overcome that she had been betrayed by her own kindred, Matthew utterly dismayed that Mistress Barfutt should have laid bare so easily the skeleton of their plot. She had been wrong with regard to the King but right in her suspicion of everyone else. 'We must go down to this mill,' the officer continued. 'This,' he said, tapping the letter in his hands, 'this points to the fact that the King may not be involved, but even if he has escaped the net, we have almost as fine a bird to snare in Master Miller.'

Mistress Barfutt was oddly subdued in her victory, for matters had been taken too far out of her hands. She did not look at her cousin as she was made ready for the ride and led outside to the waiting horses, nor at Matthew, who was hoisted into the saddle of his borrowed pony. She went to one of the barns and began preparing her market cart for hurried use.

When they left the farm, Matthew rode awkwardly, because his hands were still bound. He kept his head high, his eyes fixed on the pony's twitching ears in front. It was the indignity of his capture which rankled most — not that he was a prisoner with an uncovered plot and little hope, but that he had been made to look ridiculous. The fall among the pans — if he had had the sense to keep the letter it might have remained undiscovered — the great jackboot in the small of his back and the giggle at the sight of his stew-spattered clothes. His cheeks burned at the memory and because the smell of onions and seasoned gravy continued to rise to his nostrils from his stained garments.

It was probably the last time he would ever journey from Virgin Farm to Christchurch between the two rivers; he

would never see the mill or Master Hogg again. He wondered if the two men sensed the danger that was moving towards them. Master Hogg, after the ambush of the night, should guess at the possibility, but the miller would be waiting for an answer to his letter, and a troop of Cromwellian soldiery would be the unexpected reply. Matthew watched the road as it disappeared under the horses' hoofs. It was all so familiar; he knew every bush, every curve, even the ruts, and the bend which went into a pool of water, the hedge where the hips were ripest, the patch of stubby red candles made by the cuckoo pint berries, the sweep of the river and the pasture where a brown and white cow always stood alone, swishing her tail and gazing with melting eyes at the passers-by. A shiver ran down his spine; the familiar objects were approaching too quickly and soon the walls of the castle would come into sight.

He glanced ahead at Hester, who rode, head bowed, behind one of the troopers. By her attitude she could have been praying; under the circumstances both Giles and Nicholas, with the ingrained habit of their upbringing, would have done the same, probably not in words approved of by the Puritan Government, but in a form which satisfied their faith. Matthew could think of nothing but the words of the Litany which his brother had forced him to repeat. As he momentarily closed his eyes, a hand caught roughly at his shoulder and an amused voice told him that 'there was time enough to swoon when he reached the castle'. Angrily he jerked the hand away, and for the rest of the journey remained rigidly upright in the saddle.

The cavalcade swung left into the castle gates. Although some of the walls were crumbling and ill-kept, the keep was strong, with guns mounted on it. There were exchanges between the Constable of the castle and the officer, the former expressing surprise that the little-used building was required once more as a prison. He evidently thought at first, by his apologetic manner, that it was an armed force come to see why the Government orders for the dismantling of the fortress had not been carried out. He fumbled through keys, mumbling that there was no place fit to put a woman, and eventually Hester was assisted from her horse and escorted by the Constable's wife into their own home nearer the river.

Matthew expected no such considerate treatment for himself, nor was he given it. He was dragged from the pony and propelled towards the steps leading up to the keep.

'This way, scullion,' mocked the soldier guiding him. 'Maybe we can find some more greasy pans for you to scour, after you've had a rest in there.'

He kicked a door with his foot and gave Matthew a push into the darkness. Matthew slipped on slime-covered steps, lost his balance and rolled into an evil-smelling pool at the bottom. A guffaw of laughter reached his ears as the heavy door was bolted. In a fury he staggered to his feet, slithered on the stairs and tried to beat his bound arms against the unresisting wood. At that moment he hated the Cromwellian soldiers, hated all who had taken from him his home, driven his parents abroad and his brother to probable death. He tried to shout that he was better than they—he had his own horses, his falcon, his uncle had a library of books—that they were nothing more than a crowd of rebels who had murdered their own King, that he would escape and go to France and one day, it did not matter how many years ahead, he would return and mock and torment them as he had been mocked and tormented.

But it was no use beating a door he could not see, with arms he could not use, lowering himself still further by ill-mannered shouting at boorish soldiers. Giles would have maintained his dignity. At the thought of his brother, Matthew sank down and leaned in dejection against the damp wall. The fate of Giles and Nicholas was unknown; Mistress Hester was a prisoner as he was; Master Hogg and the miller, he felt, were able to take care of themselves, but there was still the timid little sister of Nicholas, for whom he had felt such contempt.

'Poor Katharine,' he murmured. 'What is going to happen to her?'

In his own miserable situation, he found himself wishing that he could go to her aid, and so make up for his past unchivalrous behaviour.

Chapter XVII

The Merchant and the Miller

'KATE!'

Katharine stirred as the sound of her name slid into her dreams. She was warm and comfortable, still rolled in the blankets in which Nicholas had carried her up to bed. As she drifted into wakefulness, some remembrance of the previous night swept back into her mind—the empty loft above Mistress Tuck's cottage, the boats by the dark water, the tumult of the run and, finally, Nicholas holding her tightly.

'Kate!' This time her shoulder was shaken gently.

'Nick,' she murmured.

'It is not Nicholas and you must get up.'

Katharine opened her eyes, to see the miller bending over her.

'It is early yet,' he went on, 'and I know you have had little sleep, but this day must not appear different from any other. Master Hogg will want his breakfast, Mistress Tuck will come as usual and must be told that your brother is hiding in the mill. They must, somehow, be rowed down to Mudeford and wait there until we can find Matthew—we have no more than twenty-four hours, for I had hoped to have them sail on the morning tide tomorrow.'

'Tomorrow, for France?' Katharine sat up.

'It is for their own safety that they should go so soon,' he replied. 'Here are your clothes.' He placed the garments Nicholas had stripped from her on the end of the bed. 'The most I can say is that they are dry,' he added, as he went out closing the door quietly behind him.

Katharine wriggled from the blankets and pulled the clothes towards her. They were crumpled, and streaky where the dye had run with the water, the gown and petticoats were a shade duller, there were stockings, but no shoes. Those must have been washed from her feet in the current. She dressed quickly, knotting the cut lacing of her bodice and tugging it across her chest because the woollen cloth had shrunk with the hasty drying. Her hair was tangled and the teeth of the comb snapped as she pulled it viciously through the strands. Always after it had been washed, Hester had spent hours softly curling and brushing it into shape; now, with no Hester, no brush and no curling pins, Katharine found that it hung like a fluffy curtain over her face, crackling wildly if she tried to smooth it behind her ears.

When she went down to the living-room, she saw that the miller and Master Hogg were already seated at the bare table, engrossed in discussing the different fish to be found in the rivers.

'Sniggles,' the miller was saying. 'That is the name for eels here, sniggles.'

'Sniggles or eels,' Katharine thought; what did it matter on that day that was to be the same as all the others, but which was so very different, with Giles and Nicholas hidden in the mill and Master Hogg to be deceived. Looking at the two men it seemed impossible to believe that she had seen them in such unlikely circumstances only a few hours earlier. The lean miller listening intently to Master Hogg's information did not give the impression of a powerful swimmer. Master Hogg, lolling in his chair, his jovial face beaming with interest, was not at all like the sharp little man with the lantern on the beach. A vague doubt began to grow in Katharine's mind, for she alone had cast the first suspicion on the merchant.

She hurried to the dresser and reached for plates, tankards and knives to put on the table; bread from the cupboard, butter, honey, salt—she counted them over to herself. The miller would draw the ale when they wanted it, and there was a basket of fruit on the ledge under the window. She cut thick slices from the ham she had cooked herself—sweetening it with honey and spices, soaking it in cider and boiling it until the skin peeled easily from the rich, white flesh. She could not help admiring the pink and white, and the gold of the breadcrumbs, but there was no time for day-dreaming; there were eggs to fry in the pan over the fire. As she took the last four eggs from the bowl, she thought how much more convenient it would be if the miller had his own hens and vegetable garden, instead of having to rely on Mistress Tuck.

Katharine wriggled the hot fat in the pan and glanced at Master Hogg, who had grown weary of waiting for his eggs and was cutting three neat slivers from the ham on his plate. At the sound, the three cats appeared, paws stretched, tails waving, and watched hopefully. The white-faced one stood on her hind legs, her little pink mouth open for the delicacy to drop in; the tabby crouched like a huge furry ball, and the ginger purred, weaving a pattern between Master Hogg's legs and the table. It paused, sniffing inquisitively at an unfamiliar object. The fat spattered on to Katharine's fingers as she, too, saw the unfamiliar object—Master Hogg was armed. The long, thin sheath of his sword hung from his belt and nestled against his body. All the time he had been at the mill he had never before carried a weapon.

Katharine crossed the room quickly, trembling with fear as she ladled the eggs from the pan. She broke three and apologized for her clumsiness. She took her own simple breakfast back to the hearth, where she could watch Master Hogg unnoticed. Usually in a hurry, often saddling his horse before the miller had finished his meal, on the morning when they both wished him out of their sight he was relaxed and leisured, as if the whole day stretched before him.

'I have a long day ahead,' the miller remarked, as if struck by the same thought. 'I'll not join you and Mistress Tuck at midday, Kate. You can take some bread and cheese into the mill for me now and I will eat it when I have the time. Will you be with us?' He glanced up at the merchant.

'Possibly, I am in no hurry,' Master Hogg replied.

'If you have finished, Kate,' the miller continued, seeing the untouched bread upon her plate, 'it will help me if you go over the list of grain I have handled this month. I will write a rough inventory and it should tally with the one on the bench in the mill.'

Hoping that she had not shown her stupidity, for she scarcely understood what he was talking about, Katharine pushed her food on one side and waited, full of curiosity and apprehension, for his next instructions. The miller left the table and without troubling to sit down drew pen and paper from the dresser and began to write across the sheet. His hand made two distinct columns. Katharine paid little attention, but Master Hogg's eyes followed every stroke, as if trying to read the words by the movement of the quill. The miller straightened his back, folded the paper and slipped it between the slices of bread on the board, and placed a large piece of cheese on the top.

'Correct it if it is wrong,' he said, and returned to the table.

Master Hogg cleared his throat. 'Mills and bread are such an everyday part of our lives—in fact, one might say an essential part of our lives, for we could not do without them.' He rubbed a crust thoughtfully through the broken egg on his plate. 'There must be many like myself, who have seen the wheel churning in the water, yet never seen the machinery which it drives——'

Katharine's fingers tightened on the platter, for she knew instinctively what he was going to say. Fortunately, he was not looking at her or he would have seen the dismayed expression; he was staring at the miller, whose features were under control.

'I should like to watch you at your work today, Master Miller,' he announced cheerfully.

'When you please, as soon as the meal is ended,' the miller agreed. He cut himself another slice of ham and buttered his bread slowly.

Katharine fled, down the steps and into the empty mill. She set the food on the bench and crouched on the floor, feverishly turning over the layers of papers to find the one she wanted.

'I must do as he says,' she murmured. 'But how he can think of lists of corn when they are still in the mill and Master Hogg is coming in at any minute, I don't understand.'

She found the list for September and opened her own to compare them. 'Four sacks of barley-meal' appeared at the top of each in the miller's spidery hand. The next item on hers read, 'take food', and in the opposite column, 'to your brother'. Katharine stared and began again. It was the oddest inventory she had ever seen, for interspersed with sacks of peas and corn were instructions for her to carry out—the original list only contained the peas and corn. They were to hide in the barge below the jetty; Mistress Tuck was to tow the barge at once down to Mudeford; if the great water-wheel stopped turning, that was the signal for immediate danger and they could expect no more help from the miller.

Katharine did not waste any more time. Taking the paper and the platter, she ran up the stairs to the granary.

'Nick, Nick,' she whispered, as she peered among the bins in the dark room.

Two heads were cautiously raised above the sacks in the farthest corner and she darted towards them. She pushed the paper and food into their hands and tried to explain what they were to do.

'Master Hogg will not leave him,' she went on, 'and he is wearing a sword—he has never worn one before, and you must go. Please go quickly,' she implored.

'The barge is below this window, if it is the one I saw last night when we swam up,' Giles muttered, eating hastily while he talked. He crumpled the miller's list and put it in his pocket. 'Better on me than you,' he said to Katharine, 'and better out of the mill than in. The miller will need all his wits about him to delude Master Hogg, and if I can reach

Mudeford I must look for Matthew myself. Twenty-four hours —it is not long, when most of it is daylight.'

Nicholas had gone to the window. 'Cold, uninviting water,' he remarked, on seeing the sack-laden barge rolling heavily on the slow, grey swell. 'There are several bales of rushes which should hide us effectively. It is no use trying the door,' he added, as Katharine made a move towards it. 'That is too near Master Hogg and his breakfast. It will have to be this window.'

Giles was already searching the rubbish and knotting together any odd pieces of rope and sack that he could find, making a length of several thicknesses. He wound one end round the shaft which came up through the floor and tested its strength.

'Will you go first?' he asked Nicholas.

Nicholas nodded, and suddenly taking his sister in his arms, kissed her. 'Until I return from France with a victorious King,' he whispered. He straddled the sill, twisted the rope between his legs and slipped out of sight.

Giles watched his progress. 'He will have to jump, it is not nearly long enough,' he commented. 'Now, Kate,' he turned to her, 'when I have gone, haul in the rope, untie it and bury it in one of these hutches. We don't want Master Hogg to see it.' He sat on the sill, smiling, but more matter-of-fact than Nicholas. 'We could not have managed without you, Katharine,' he said gratefully. 'Hester will see you safely home, and in time, no doubt, we shall be able to write from wherever we are.' He squeezed through the window and slid down the rope.

Katharine leaned out. It was all happening too quickly for her to feel any pain. At that moment it was their safety that mattered most. She caught a glimpse of Nicholas kneeling on the jetty and Giles springing to his side as the rope slackened between her fingers. She pulled it in, uncoiled it from the shaft and thrust it, arm deep, into one of the bins, as she had been told. Working methodically through her instructions, she spread the remaining bread and cheese over the platter and took it with her to the room below and placed it on the bench. She went outside on to the landing-stage. The barge lay low in the heavy water and in the distance, round the bend in the river, Mistress Tuck's little boat was creeping towards the mill. Katharine's feet tapped impatiently on the wooden boards and she tugged at her knotted bodice strings, for there was still the last part of her message to deliver — the frightening warning that the stopping of the mill was the end of all hope, and the instructions that the fugitives were to be hidden on the marsh, for the miller could do no more.

Seeing the restless figure standing there, Mistress Tuck quickened her strokes, and as the boat glided under the jetty, Katharine held the prow and drew it in close.

'I'm late,' the widow said, shipping her oars. 'The tide is nearly on the turn. Does he know there were soldiers at the harbour mouth last night?'

Katharine nodded, and kneeling by the boat, in a swift whisper tried to tell what had happened. Mistress Tuck, looking grave, glanced behind her to where the miller and Master Hogg were hovering on the steps. 'You'd best stay with him, Kate,' she murmured. 'It will look odd if you come too, and he may need your help.'

She nodded 'Good day' as Master Hogg strolled nearer and pointed at the barge. 'Some of yours?' he asked the miller.

'Barley-meal and rushes for Portsmouth,' the miller replied, bending over the penstock across the mill stream. Slowly the hatch was raised, the water rushed through and the great wheel began to turn.

The three of them entered the mill. Master Hogg, eager and interested like a child, peering into the corners and prodding sacks with his boot, clattered up the stairs to the room above. The miller started hoisting the bags by the pulley in the ceiling and Katharine, who was last, paused behind the closed half-door to listen. Above the rumbling of the machinery she heard the uneven trample of horses' hoofs. White-faced, she moved to the miller.

'Keep near me and do as I tell you,' he muttered.

Master Hogg suddenly reappeared on the stairs, looking amazed and incredulous. 'What is happening?' he demanded angrily.

He had scarcely finished speaking before there was a noise like a mighty, thunderous wind, the door burst open and a horde of Cromwellian soldiers swept across the room. They saw only the merchant, standing alone and exposed, on the darkened stairway.

'That is Hogg,' someone shouted. 'Cut him down!'

With a bellow of fury Master Hogg whipped out his sword from its sheath and disarmed his first assailant.

'What foolery is this?' he roared. 'What idiot has sent you to arrest me? I am no spy—I am the Government agent from Lymington.'

In the babel and confusion that followed the miller stooped swiftly and slid the dropped sword into his own hand; with the other he slammed the door again and shot the bolt. Katharine was appalled; all the time she had been whispering desperately to herself that it was the opportunity for them to escape.

'We have got to keep them here, Kate,' the miller muttered, seeing her frightened look. 'Is the barge moving?'

She murmured a hoarse and choked 'Yes'. Crouching against the wall she could see the line of the river, and the barge, like a long, black slug, creeping inch by inch past the end of the jetty.

'That is the man you want, the miller of Place,' Master Hogg's voice rose above the din. 'He is responsible for the King's escape. I have troopers expected from Lymington within the hour to search the whole town.'

With a hum of excitement the men swung round, and to Katharine, cowering behind the miller, it was like the sea—a pounding sea of noise, with the wheel rumbling on, the sack

swaying on the pulley and the dark faces, dark uniforms and flashing blades. She was almost as much terrified by the change in the miller and Master Hogg; once more they had been transformed from quiet men with whom she had spent many peaceful days into creatures of strength and steel.

Master Hogg forced a path through the struggling mass jammed in the tiny, cramped space, his wrist striking like a snake with a silver tongue as he attacked the miller.

'I'll wager you are a better swordsman than grinder of corn, Master Miller,' he panted, as he found he was unable to break the other's guard.

'And I'll wager you know more of warfare than merchant shipping,' the miller retorted. 'Kate,' he spoke quietly, his eyes fixed on the wavering points in front of him. 'When I shout, I can hold them no longer; run for the stream and drop the hatch. You understand?'

Katharine, sickened by the sight of one man already wounded nearly being trampled under his companions' feet, and the blood rushing from a cut on the miller's shoulder, understood only too well. She edged to the door and curled her fingers on the bolt.

'Now!' As the miller cried the word, he flicked his sword upwards. The blade ripped the sack hanging on the pulley and a shower of blinding, choking flour descended, covering the soldiers and clouding the whole room. In that one defenceless moment, the miller's weapon was twisted from his grasp, and Master Hogg's, under the shock and weight of the meal, went spinning to the floor.

Katharine saw only the merchant, white from head to foot, his eyes blazing from his coughing, contorted face, as he grappled, bare-handed, with the miller, who barred the way out.

She sped through the door, across the cobbles to the penstock behind the wheel. Putting all her strength to the winch, she heaved until the hatch rattled into place and the swift flow of the stream was stopped. There was sudden, complete silence. Then, on her knees beside the mill-race, she was conscious of the sounds beginning again—the water dripping, the trees in the wind, the goat champing the grass, and horses thudding in the lane to the mill. Through eyes blurred with tears, she watched the tiny figure of Mistress Tuck, in the walnut shell of a boat, drawing the laden barge into the distance of the open river.

Chapter XVIII

A Departure and a Return

KATHARINE was raised to her feet by one of the horsemen who had just arrived. None of them troubled about the silent mill, for its noise had only made conversation more difficult. She was led back to the cobbles and there, because the living-room was too small to contain them all, were assembled the two separate troops of Cromwellian soldiers, Mistress Barfutt's from Ringwood, Master Hogg's from Lymington.

Master Hogg appeared through the doorway of the mill talking to the officers in charge, beating his dusty garments and shaking his powdered head like a dog from the water. Behind him, was the miller, a rag stuffed in his shirt to cover the cut, which scarcely seemed to worry him, and his arms held by two troopers. His eyes met Katharine's and he smiled, a gesture which reassured her, for if he could still smile there must be some hope. Master Hogg, as if he felt the interrogation was going to be lengthy, called for the table and stools to be brought from indoors. Before he had time to sit down, there was the rattle of a cart in the lane and into the crowded yard drove Mistress Barfutt. She knotted the reins over the pony's neck and climbed down.

'I have come to get my dues,' she announced.

Master Hogg glared at her. 'Dues?' He spat out the word with venom. 'This has all been your doing, I imagine.' He advanced upon her with a slow, stalking gait. 'You set a false trail in order to have me removed so that your schemes to help the King might be furthered, you sent for troops from Ringwood and arranged for them to arrive after your supposed servants had left the farm, you planned for the boy Matthew to work for me and spy on all I did—you shall have your dues. Put her under arrest,' he snapped.

As the hand descended on Mistress Barfutt's arm, she shook it off contemptuously. 'Lies!' she exclaimed. 'Nothing but lies! I sent for soldiers as soon as my Cousin Hester arrived from Gloucester, because I suspected the servants and the sick child, who had nothing the matter with her. One of the men could have been the King, he was very like, and the other could have been this child's brother——'

'And I nearly had those two men in my hands last night,' Master Hogg interrupted. 'Someone warned them of the danger and I'll wager you were at the bottom of it.'

Mistress Barfutt ignored him and pointed at Katharine. 'She is no more the miller's niece than I am. She comes from a well known Royalist family who——'

'Then what is she doing here?' Master Hogg broke in again, giving Katharine a quick look.

'She ran away.'

He laughed. 'Do you expect me to believe that? A child, a stranger to these parts, runs away and conveniently finds the hide-out of a man we had long thought had escaped to France? It is much more probable that you sent her, that your cousin requested your aid as she had a pair of fugitives on her hands, and that the child was the link between the mill and the farm, to spy on me—yes,' Master Hogg remembered his map, 'to spy on me, when the boy could not.'

'She was the weak link in their chain,' Mistress Barfutt retorted. 'She ran away because she had not the courage to go on pretending to be ill. You ask her who her father was and why he was shot, and then you will know why she ran away.'

The miller's swift movement of protest was checked by his guards. Master Hogg turned to Katharine with an abrupt 'Well?'

The trooper who had his arm around her shoulder, partly holding her prisoner and partly to give her some courage, for he could feel her trembling under the gaze of so many eyes, tapped her cheek with his finger at her silence. 'You'd better answer,' he murmured. 'It won't do to keep him waiting.'

Katharine obeyed, head bowed to hide her unsteady lips.

'He was Colonel Sir Edward Lambert,' she replied flatly, 'and he was shot because he was a traitor, by the Royalists, in the garden at home.'

'And now ask her who bore the litter all the way from the north,' went on Mistress Barfutt, undeterred by the lack of reaction to the information.

This time Katharine needed more help than the trooper could give her and she looked in despair at the miller. He was watching her intently and with the slightest inclination of his head told her what to say.

'It—it was Nicholas,' she stammered, at Master Hogg's repeated impatient bark. 'Nicholas, my brother, and Matthew and Giles, his brother, and—and I warned them not to cross the run last night—and I put the boat out and it upset and we were all in the water and—please need you ask me any more?' she entreated, and covering her face with the bedraggled skirt of her dress, she fought back the rising tears.

Master Hogg stroked his chin thoughtfully, looked with little liking at Mistress Barfutt, with suspicion at the miller and with doubt at his fellow officers.

'Drowned?' he queried, raising his eyebrows.

'Possibly,' one answered quietly. 'She is not lying.'

'Katharine,' Master Hogg said, in a gentler tone than he had used before. 'I want you to answer one more question. Did Mistress Barfutt send you to the mill, or is she speaking the truth when she says you ran away?' He removed her hands from her face so that she could not avoid his eyes.

'I ran away,' she whispered, 'but——'

'But not for the reason she gave,' he finished the sentence.

'You need not be afraid to tell me, you will not be betraying the miller, for we know who he is. We knew he re-took your home in Gloucester, that he ordered your father's execution, and that for his political and military conspiracies against the Government, he has become a much wanted man.'

Katharine did not hear any more. In the mist before her, she saw, not the mill and the grey, clouded sky, but a vivid scene with jet black shadows on the sunlit stones; she saw her father's kneeling figure, Nicholas's face, scarlet with shame, and herself, running across the courtyard, and then, the tall, brown man with the blue eyes, who carried her to the women on the terrace. He had smiled then, to comfort her, but he was not smiling now as she stared across the cobbles, for he had no comfort to give. He had pieced her story together so easily when she came to the mill, that she had thought in her fear she must have told him everything, not that he already knew it. He had not wanted to meet Nicholas, who, although disowning his father, might not have welcomed his executioner; and Mistress Tuck had said that he had a liking for her which was not merely because her brother was a fugitive hiding at the farm. During those short days at the mill, Katharine thought, he had so adequately filled the place of the man he had taken away, and now she could do nothing to help him, except to try to show that her confidence was unshaken, even after learning who he was.

Gravely, she turned back to Master Hogg, who was waiting for her answer. She told him that Mistress Barfutt had only hoped to capture the King because she wanted the reward to pay for a new barn and dairy. She told him that Hester knew nothing of their plans, because she was unable to speak with Nicholas, that Matthew had, all along, only obeyed his brother, and that she was the one who had disobeyed. She had gone her own way, and because of that, she was as guilty as the miller.

It was Master Hogg who was smiling when she had finished,

a sad, meditative smile. He sat down at the table and drew pen and paper towards him.

'These are your orders,' he said bluntly, to the other officers. 'Half your men are to go to Mudeford and search the area. If, by dusk, they have found no trace of Nicholas Lambert and his friend—it is possible that they were both drowned and that we are wasting time and troops, who are needed elsewhere—then the boy Matthew may be released from the castle. The woman, Mistress Hester, is to be conducted under escort to her home in Gloucester, with instructions to the Governor of the county that she is not to leave it again under any pretext whatsoever. For the moment, this child Katharine Lambert is to be lodged in the castle, too, and Mistress Barfutt.' His pen stabbed across the page as he wrote the words. 'But, when Mistress Barfutt is released, she is to return to Virgin and concern her mind in future solely with affairs of the farm. And the miller,' he continued softly, as he spoke of the man who had deceived him completely, 'the miller, if he still wishes to be referred to as such, knows that his past activities have earned him the penalty of death.' He paused significantly. 'But, as that decision does not rest with me, and may be commuted to imprisonment for life, he shall be housed in Hurst Castle outside Lymington, there to await the sentence of a higher authority.'

As he said the words, Katharine saw in her mind his map, propped on the stool under the window, and the thin lines he had drawn for the shingle bank running out to the lonely fortress in the sea.

'Do you wish to speak with her?' Master Hogg's abrupt question was directed at the miller.

Although his guards released him immediately, the miller did not move, until Katharine, putting out her hands impulsively, made a quick step nearer. He took her cold fingers between his warm ones, and looked searchingly into her hazel eyes.

'I did not want you to know so much, Kate,' he said, very

quietly, so that his voice could not be heard beyond the two of them, 'and I can only ask you not to have bitterness for the past. For the present you need have no fear—' he smiled, as if willing into her some of his own faith—'and for the future—there is always hope. Good-bye, Mistress Mouse.'

He turned and went back to his guards. 'I am ready,' he said.

They fetched his coat from a nail in the mill and saddled his horse in the stable. Master Hogg, with evident respect for his prisoner, allowed him to mount unbound and, taking his place at his side, directed the party of troopers to the lane and the road to Lymington.

Katharine was put in the cart with Mistress Barfutt, and they trundled through the grey morning up to the castle in Christchurch. She saw nothing of the route, nor the soldiers in the yard, nor the house into which she was taken. She hardly saw her cousin Hester, who, with a cry of pleasure and relief, ran to greet her as the Constable's wife led in the two extra prisoners. A few weeks earlier Katharine would have welcomed the caressing arms and would have cried out her unhappiness on her cousin's shoulder, but now, it was an unhappiness too deep to be shared. She forced a smile, suffered the eager embrace, and went to stand alone at the window overlooking the mill-stream, for the second loss was almost too much for her to bear.

'She was like that when her father was killed,' Hester murmured in unnecessary explanation to Mistress Barfutt, because she, herself, was unable to understand the girl's behaviour. 'We gave her toys and stuffed her mouth with sweets, but not a word would she say.'

To Katharine, half listening to their conversation, it was beyond her understanding that, only a few hours before, one of the women, through her greed, had caused the other's arrest, and now, they were confiding in each other and finding solace in a common trouble.

Hester had not known all her cousin's disloyalty and was ready to forgive, and Mistress Barfutt did not intend that she should learn any more of what she had done. With a red face and flustered manner, she made out that Hester's arrest was as much a mistake as her own had been, and, after taking sidelong glances at Katharine, she was of the opinion that the child, because of her distress, would not have the courage to denounce her to her cousin. It was impossible for Hester, at that moment, to know the full truth, because she had not been present at the arrival of the soldiers in the kitchen, nor had she been present at the interrogation at the mill. At the memory of what had happened at the mill, Mistress Barfutt's fingers twitched with the desire to catch the plump little merchant by the scruff of his neck. He had given her no credit for attempting to capture the King, and no credit for helping towards the arrest of the miller, but he had humiliated her and, after all her scheming, she was left with nothing more than she had before—an old barn and a small dairy.

On the fate of Giles and Nicholas both the women had the wisdom to remain silent. Hester dared not question Katharine because, all through the long day, they were never allowed to be on their own. It was not until after dark, that the three prisoners were told by the Constable's wife that they were free to go, because no trace of the fugitives had been found. To Katharine only, did the news mean more than release, for she knew then that her brother and Giles were hidden at Mudeford, waiting for the morning when the miller's prearranged boat would sail them to France and safety.

Mistress Barfutt took an affectionate farewell of her cousin in the torch-lit castle yard, and climbed into her pony cart. Hester was to stay for the rest of the night, after which a trooper would be ready to accompany her to Gloucester. She naturally expected Katharine to stay with her, but Katharine, with a firmness she had not shown before, said that she wished to see Mistress Tuck, who had been so kind to her and who would want to know what had happened at the mill. It was impossible for her to say more, because they were surrounded by the Constable, his wife and the soldiers. Hester, with great reluctance, for she had no idea who the woman was nor where she lived, but hoping there was more to Katharine's request than appeared, allowed her to go. It was Matthew's timely release that alleviated her mind. He was brought from the keep, dirty, his garments reeking, with no joy in his freedom for he was friendless and in complete ignorance of all that had occurred. Hester approached him, where he stood in the shadows fingering the bridle of his pony, which had been returned to him.

'Go with Katharine to see this woman,' she begged. 'It is not safe for her to be alone in the town at this hour, nor should she be running about in her stockinged feet. In the morning you shall come back with us to Gloucester and from there to your uncle again.'

Back to his uncle in Shropshire, Matthew thought grimly, with the books and the horses and the falcon. Somehow, he did not want them any longer; he wanted Giles and his parents and a sunny home in France. He mounted obediently and pulled the small Katharine with ease across the saddle in front of him. He put an arm round her waist to hold her securely and with the other took the reins.

'Which way? ' he asked, as the pony reached the castle gate.

'Mudeford,' she whispered, so softly that he had to bend his ear to her lips. 'Mudeford, where they are safe.'

In Mistress Tuck's heavily shuttered cottage they were reunited with Giles and Nicholas. The village, the woods and the marsh had been searched, but the barge, which had been watched while the barley-meal was unloaded until it only appeared to contain rushes and empty sacks, had been left untouched, floating on the tides with the other small craft in the placid harbour.

'A boat will be on the beach before dawn,' Mistress Tuck said, as she began to tell them of the arrangements for their escape. 'I saw the master of the vessel today, when the miller could not meet him. It was him who saw to the unloading of the barge, and a fine job he made of it, with the soldiers poking every sack he put on the jetty. The boat will take you to the coaster off the Island,' she continued, 'and that will change course to drop you somewhere off the French shore. I can't say where.'

'France,' Matthew breathed the word with pleasure.

'It may not be all you imagine,' Giles warned him. 'We shall be poor, at the court of an exiled king, living on the charity of others, and many will treat us with disdain.'

'I would rather disdain from foreigners than from my own countrymen,' Matthew replied, remembering his recent humiliation.

'But we must fight to return,' Nicholas interrupted. 'The King must be restored, our freedom is for that purpose. That is the least we can do for the man who has helped us and who has given his freedom, possibly his life, in exchange for ours.'

'You saw his letter, Matthew, who was he?' Giles asked.

Katharine started from the fireside where she had been sitting, still only half conscious of what was going on around her, but realizing that it was she, not Matthew, who ought to tell Nicholas.

'He was the man who had our father shot as a traitor,' she said bluntly.

The silence was frightening. Nicholas, as his closely guarded secret of six years was flung among them, made a hasty movement towards his sister, checked himself and remained staring at her across the room. Controlling his anger, he said very quietly, 'In the morning, Katharine, Mistress Tuck will be able to see that you are at the castle in time to accompany our cousin to Gloucester.'

'I am not going,' Katharine replied. There was no defiance in her answer. She said the words simply, with determination behind them.

Nicholas, looking at her, forgot the others in the room and saw only his sister, who had changed. She was not the plump baby trying to understand an elder brother, she was not the freckle-faced, nervous girl of the journey. The open air days at the mill had given her colour, and the miller had given her something more, he thought; she had learnt confidence and self-possession, and almost over night she had grown up.

'Do you want to come to France with me?' he asked.

'I am going back to the mill,' she said. 'I am going to the mill with Mistress Tuck, and somehow, between us, we shall keep it working. Nicholas, please,' she clasped his fingers eagerly and hurried on to avoid interruption. 'He may not be killed, Master Hogg said that. They may set him free in time or when the King comes back, and it will give him something to live for—some hope—if he knows the wheel is still turning and we are waiting for him. He—he said there was hope for the future.' Her eyes searched his for some indication of his feelings.

Mistress Tuck rose quietly. She had known nothing of Katharine's suggestion, but she stood with her in front of Nicholas. 'I would dearly like to return to Place,' she said. 'Your sister would be safe with me, and I can hire a man to do the heavy work, he need not know much, I taught the—other all he knew. His hope is as slender as a thread of gossamer,' she spoke softly in the hushed room, 'but I've seen gossamer on the autumn mornings being blown by the wind, and the little spider creatures clinging to it—and it holds. If he's something to cling to in the years of darkness in Hurst, something to give him hope, then I will help him to it.'

Nicholas turned his sister's hands over and over in his. He ran his fingers over the fair hairs and over the faint lines on her palms, while he struggled with his thoughts.

'It will not be a life to which you have been accustomed,' he said, at length. 'But I know there are too many bitter memories at the house in Gloucester. You may stay, Kate, but only on one condition.' He felt by the tightening of her muscles that the condition would have to be convincing. 'I am your only near relation—your guardian, in fact—and it is not wise that we should be separated.' He smiled. 'If Mistress Tuck will allow, I will be your miller, and live with you at Place.'

No one made any attempt to dissuade him, least of all, Giles. He and Matthew had parents and a home to go to abroad, and it was only right that Nicholas should build his new life in company with his sister. By the morning, the area would be emptied of soldiers, the castle would contain no one but the Constable and his wife, and the guns he was too lazy to move; the carters would not question a new face at the mill with Mistress Tuck cleaning in the usual way—the news of the previous miller's arrest would have already spread—and Christchurch would once more be the sleepy little fisher town.

Only Hester would have to remain in ignorance of their whereabouts until Nicholas could send her a letter, and it would not be a pleasant journey for her, travelling alone and distressed, under guard, to the lodge in Gloucester.

They had no rest that night, and while it was still dark and the sea scarcely awake, with limp waves breaking along the shore, they crept down to the beach, where a boat was waiting. Mistress Tuck handed the man the bag of money which the miller had left with her, and held up two fingers as only Giles and Matthew waded forward and climbed into the stern. The man nodded, slipped the oars into the water and edged out into the open sea. The small craft, on the grey swell in the grey light, was almost invisible, as was the little group huddled on the shingle, their hands raised in farewell.

An hour later, when the yellow and blue of the dawn had broken over the horizon, Nicholas, Katharine and Mistress Tuck rowed through the shallow harbour and up the river. On the mudbanks which the tide had washed bare, the gulls were dancing, hoping to deceive the worms into thinking that the water was trickling back; the dry reeds stirred in the wind, and the tiny creeks, empty and silent, wound like sandy tracks between the exposed roots. Katharine stared ahead to the mill, sheltering under the trees of the Priory. Beside the jetty, in the overgrown garden, she caught a glimpse of a horned, white face.

'The goat will need milking,' she said quietly, 'and I must learn how to do it.'

It was a relief, after the tense departure of Giles and Matthew, to be able to speak of something so ordinary.

'Ay,' Mistress Tuck murmured, 'it was never the Lord's way that the world should stand still—and the wheel shall be turning too, within the hour.'

She smiled at Nicholas and Katharine, for, after the years of loneliness, she had been given, in them, what she had always lacked.

Above them, the sky was clear, October blue, and already the sun was creeping down the walls of the mill, as somewhere out at sea it was glistening on the rigging of the coasting vessel, and, on the spit of yellow shingle, it was slowly warming the bleak stones of Hurst Castle.

THE END

PRINTED IN GREAT BRITAIN BY
NORTHUMBERLAND PRESS LIMITED
GATESHEAD ON TYNE